His Cold Kiss

Cyborg Redemption

By Michelle Howard

Published by MH Publications

Prologue

Standing in line behind dozens of his cyborg brethren in the multi-level auditorium, Cyllus increased the suppression on his emotions to control his rage. The trial to charge him and the others was a complete sham. There had been no investigation, no questions into why he and members of the Military Elite had done what they'd done and launched a full scale rebellion.

Now he stood to be sentenced for going against orders. The wrists and ankle cuffs clinked as he took another step forward. Attempting to hack them or steal a key was pointless, considering the guards surrounding them.

Jeers and threats rained down on him along with the low rumble of conversation his auditory enhancements couldn't quite make out.

The crowd of onlookers composed of his fellow citizens of Kirs exhibited a wide range of emotions. Confusion, anger and fear displayed prominently on their faces. Cyllus understood their feelings. With little public notice, charges had been entered to declare that the cyborgs in the Military Elite were traitors to their home world.

It was true Cyllus was one of many who began to question the emperor's orders. Not at first. He had been a loyal soldier through and through and thought his actions were justified.

Until he'd heard about a pod of cyborgs who refused an order to fire their weapons into a gathering of women and children in a small city on Bionus, a neighboring planet. The inhabitants of Bionus had never bothered those on Kirs. They each existed peacefully and blissfully unconcerned by what the other did for years.

But that all changed with the reign of the current emperor. Cyllus eyed the man responsible for his current situation. Emperor Shui. The ruler of their world was nothing like his father, the previous emperor.

After a succession of benevolent leaders in his family line, Shui, for whatever reason had let the power of his position corrupt him.

On the surface, his orders to the military had seemed legitimate. Soon though, messages looped in among Cyllus' pod on his internal closed neural network. Questions about their orders and inconsistencies in the explanations they received caused a handful to ask questions. To probe for the truth.

The only common thread cyborgs could definitively agree on was that their emperor had lied. There was no rational reason for his attempt to take over Bionus outside of greed.

At first, rumors flew within the pod groupings cyborgs were looped into. Four cyborgs made up Cyllus' pod and they shared a closed network that enabled them to communicate with stealth. Their small group had been together since they all entered the military and became cyborgs to protect and defend their world.

More and more pods questioned the truth as the emperor's lies slowly spread. They weren't fighting an honorable cause. Cyborgs were attacking innocents. Emperor Shui was using the Kirsian military force for his personal gain.

Civilians and family members became go betweens as a rebellion was born, a rebellion which picked up pace and was on track. The cyborgs would have successfully forced Emperor Shui's crimes into the light if he hadn't accidentally discovered their actions before hand. Medical techs examining the mainframe of that one pod of cyborgs reported what they found—a plethora of information about the rebellious activities from the Kirsians.

Luckily Shui only managed to get minor details from that particular pod's NNP. The rest of the cyborgs assisted in scrubbing the broader public mainframe before he could access it.

All of that created the current situation Cyllus found himself in—charged with crimes and about to be sentenced as a traitor to his world.

Making matters worse, the emperor hadn't limited this trial to the cyborgs he'd arrested. There were friends and family members charged with treason as well. Cyllus locked gazes with familiar brown eyes. His mother, Kala, clutched his younger sister, Miri, close to her chest. They'd been brought in as his accomplices.

His mother was a huge proponent for justice but she hadn't been aware of Cyllus' activities. Neither had his younger sister. That hadn't stopped the emperor.

While Cyllus didn't feel the same outpouring of love for them from before his cybernetic transformation, he did remember his devotion to both women and wanted to protect them.

Guards signaled for silence as the emperor strutted into the auditorium with his head held high. Dressed in his customary robes with a neat physique and pleasant smile, he appeared stately. There had never been a reason to distrust his leadership.

Shui approached a large dais with one of his top aides behind him. He stepped in front of the podium placed at the center of the space and activated the head mic he wore. "Today is a somber day for the world of Kirs. Rebellions have been found plotting against us. The men and women that you see before you have been found guilty—"

Cyllus stiffened at the pompous display, noticing the cyborgs chained near him doing the same. The crowd erupted.

Shouts of, "When were they given a trial? Is this legal? This isn't fair," rang out.

With a pointed look at his aide, Shui signaled that he wanted those who'd openly posed those questions and remarks detained. Cyllus gritted his teeth and clenched his fingers into fists. Suppressing his anger was near impossible in this situation.

Shui waved both of his hands above his head to silence the crowd and sent them all a jovial smile. "As I was saying, these rebels have been found guilty of conspiring against the emperor and the citizens of Kirs. They are hereby sentenced to prison, for life."

Shui ignored another round of disruption from the onlookers and the shocked shouts thrown his way. His Prime Ministers, representing each country on Kirs, eyed him in dismay. At least they had been against Shui's plans from the beginning to take over Bionus and extend his reign as emperor over the small world.

It had made things harder, though. Follow the emperor's or the Prime Ministers' directives. Cyllus eyed the rows of cyborgs in front and behind him. Who to trust had become the most prevalent question. He'd been separated from all but one member of his pod. Kelix stood to his left, expression perfectly bland but voice rigid with fury as he murmured, "I can't believe he's getting away with this."

Two of Kelix's brothers had died during the weeks of the emperor's rampage as he attempted to find the identity of every Kirsian involved in the rebellion. The loss had hit Kelix particularly hard and he fervently wished for one opportunity to be alone with the emperor.

Their pod had managed to keep Kelix from inciting more of Shui's attention so far, but it wasn't easy.

Xion and Kaito, the other two in their pod grouping, stood several rows back, bodies rigid with the same tension filling the auditorium.

"We have to play it safe. When we reach the prison moon, Tyurma, we can reconnect with the others in our pod and form a plan," Cyllus whispered back.

And they would form a plan. They couldn't let the emperor move forward with his apparent interest in taking over and conquering any planet nearby.

On stage, Emperor Shui waved off complaints. He had issued their sentence and none could sway him. All of those considered guilty were ushered out. Cyllus thought they would head straight for the ships but more horror awaited.

The emperor's additional orders filtered through to all of them, cyborgs and civilians alike. They were to be branded. Fighting would be useless. Too many guards, too many weapons aimed their way. Instant death or prison colony where they might at least find a chance to correct this injustice.

Using all of his restraint, Cyllus masked his emotions at the added humiliation. The letters CR were burned into his flesh with a chemical his nanobots could not heal. The Kirsians not in the military each received the letter R on their cheek to identify them as a part of the rebellion as well.

Unable to fully suppress his pain from the experience, Cyllus made a vow to himself.

Emperor Shui would pay.

Chapter 1

Cold. It filled his veins and poured through his circuitry as Cyllus stared at his cellmates and pushed his rage down deep. His face no longer ached from the branded letters forced on him. His mother and sister would not be so lucky. They were somewhere on another transport, in pain and suffering.

Cyllus' honor demanded retribution. He'd make sure of it.

Like cattle with little to no concern for their welfare, the guards loaded them onto the transport ships. Only thoughts of freedom and vengeance kept Cyllus from losing his control at the way they were treated.

And the icy burn of the cold he used to keep him in an unfeeling state to prevent the thoughts of going on a killing rampage.

"Not too much longer," a guard called out as he walked by their cell with an off tune whistle.

None of the guards said much after lowering the energy shield in place to keep them locked in. Any electronics or other devices they could have used their cybernetics to bypass had clearly been deactivated or turned offline. In essence, they were trapped until they reached their destination.

Cyllus shifted his gaze to the other occupants in his cell. Aside from Kelix, there were three others. Sora, one of the few female cyborgs he'd ever crossed paths with, leaned against the wall as far from the rest of them as possible. Her arms were folded over her chest, the mutinous twist to her lips speaking loudly to her feelings about all of this.

Unlike him, she made no effort to hide or suppress her emotions. Sora wasn't part of Cyllus' original pod like Kelix and hadn't spoken since being led onboard and shoved inside with them.

He eyed the other two males. Cyllus held a basic knowledge of Reo and Tagan. Both had joined the military at the same time as him and underwent their conversion to cyborg within the same time frame as well. Neither was from his pod making them virtual strangers. Potential enemies, in fact.

Then again, the same could easily be said of him. Everyone's motives were in question thanks to this cluster fuck. Familiar anger tingled up his spine.

Cold. He had to stay cold. If he thought of his family, if he thought of the emperor's actions...cold. Must stay cold.

After he became a cyborg his emotions were stunted in some regards. The ability to disconnect saved him because Cyllus knew the soldier he'd been a long time ago would have acted first and paid the price with his life.

For now, he had to impatiently bide his time.

Suspicion burned like a lead weight in his gut, though. It was clear someone had worked with the emperor and given him key information to hack cyborg hardware. It was the only way he could have gained such specific details regarding their growing rebellion.

The pod who refused to fire on that one group of Bionus citizens only gave Emperor Shui the ammunition he needed to stop the cyborgs from exposing his actions.

Cyllus didn't trust any of them aside from Kelix and was sure his friend felt the same way.

"What the fuck?!" Kelix suddenly exclaimed. "Is everyone getting this?"

Confusion flickered in their cellmates' gazes. A mental knocking at Cyllus' open mainframe declared an incoming message waited. Accessing it would leave him susceptible to others infiltrating his core. The panic in Kelix's expression and the chatter from Xion and Kaito through his neural net processor-NNP were enough for Cyllus to forego caution.

He eased his mental barrier down and the cryptic message instantly bombarded him. An urgent alert only cyborgs could access.

Cyllus focused inward, caution in every step as he replayed the data being shared and absorbed by his fellow cyborgs. A group overheard guards planning to abandon the transport and all the prisoners with it. The information wasn't specific but apparently a bomb or timed explosives were set to destroy the vessels carrying them from Kirs.

The truth hit Cyllus hard. Emperor Shui had lied once more. None of the transport ships were going to make it to Tyurma. This trip to the prison moon was a setup to rid the emperor of those he considered a hindrance to his grand plan.

More details filtered in and Cyllus scrolled through, his brain taking in the information at a rapid rate. They'd been judged and given a life sentence with no chance of survival. Now this. Death.

His first thought turned to his sister and mother. They weren't on this ship but they were branded and bound to Tyurma on another one of the prison transports.

Urgency flooded his veins and broke through the cold. Cyllus shut down his connection and locked his mainframe again. He stared at Kelix. "We have to escape."

Cyllus shifted his gaze to the other cyborgs. "None of us are from the same pod group and there is no reason we should trust one another, but in this, I think we all can agree we need to work together."

Reo, Tagan and Sora didn't hesitate. They had pod brethren in jeopardy as well as friends and family too. "Agreed."

Sora pushed off from the wall and came over to where Cyllus stood by the energy shield that prevented them from getting out of their cell. Something he couldn't decipher flashed briefly in her steel gray gaze.

"There are no tumblers or electronic locks for us to bypass," Cyllus told her as she stood staring at their only way in or out.

Sora shot an annoyed glare in his direction. "I know that!"

The others gathered close. Tagan's gravelly voice rumbled as he said, "Getting off the transport won't be an issue if we can't get out of our cell."

They could steal or hack anything with their cybernetics if a system was powered and online. The energy shield was a different construct.

Since Cyllus was still within range to connect to his pod, he reached for them on their neural network. Kelix seamlessly joined in. Xion and Kaito were on this ship but in another cell on a different level.

As soon as Cyllus viewed their thoughts, he could see the dozens of scenarios over the NNP while they frantically searched for a solution.

"If we do not survive, I plan to take as many of the emperor's scum with me," Xion finally snarled, letting the options fade away on his end.

"I do not trust Tovark," Kaito added, naming the unknown cyborg they shared a cell with. "Xion and I can overpower him easily when we get out but I'm not sure that is viable."

Cyllus firmed his lips. Though they were of equal strength and capabilities, their pod looked to him as their leader for an answer. A brief freeze frame image of Tovark appeared in his neural net.

The sharing of information wasn't uncommon and for their pod it had become an instinctive act. Cyllus saved the image for future reference. If the other cyborg hurt his brethren, he'd know exactly who to target.

"What's she doing?"

Kelix's verbal question interrupted the private conversation. Cyllus automatically transmitted what he saw to Xion and Kaito. Sora had her palm held up and out toward the energy field. The lights shimmered from gold to blue to red.

She was disrupting the energy field but he couldn't source how. Cyllus neural net processors flared as he shared information and received the same answer from Kelix, Xion, and Kaito. They didn't know how she was doing whatever it was either.

As cyborgs, they could absorb energy from electrical currents to gain power boosts in lieu of eating or speed their healing if their nanobots failed. What Sora attempted seemed more complex than that.

No matter how many ways he analyzed it, Cyllus wasn't sure another cyborg could replicate it without electrocuting themselves or frying their circuits in the process.

He sensed the moment the shielded door weakened. Reo and Tagan inhaled sharply. Their eyelids fluttered rapidly in a clear sign they communicated with their own pod on their NNP. Cyllus smirked. He and his friends were better at masking their internal communications amongst one another.

Cyllus studied Sora's face again and noted she'd lost her stoic expression. A pained grimace now twisted her mouth, lines of strain bracketing her lips. Tension held her shoulders rigid and dots of moisture glistened on her forehead.

Most cyborgs could control their physical reactions and outward signs of exertion but sometimes there was no controlling extremes.

A visual scan of her physical condition made it easy for him to determine she was in the throes of extreme pain, but Sora didn't lower her arm or turn away from the door. Like him, she obviously understood this was a do or die situation.

Breath suspended in his throat, Cyllus waited. Silence coasted along the NNP as Xion and Kaito watched her as well. Anticipation held them all on the edge.

Then it happened. The energy field flickered. Once. Twice. Cyllus stiffened. His fingers curled at his sides in clenched fists. Hope blazed and he forced back the urge to rush her. Then with a light buzz, the shielded door dropped. There one moment, then gone.

"Fuuuck!" Sora cried out, stumbling back and dropping her arm to her side.

She gasped in wrenching gulps of air then clasped her arms about her midsection with a sharp yelp. Her back shuddered. She muffled her heavy breathing by clamping her lips tight and they all tensed. Was she malfunctioning? What if she'd damaged herself permanently in her efforts to free them?

Again, impatience flared. She needed to collect herself. Time was ticking and they needed to go.

Seconds later, Sora forced herself upright with a garbled growl. Her gray eyes sparked with fire as she took in their quiet forms studying her. Cyllus ran another visible scan. This time, he used his retinal implants, noting her pale and trembling body in the gray and black uniform of the Military Elite.

Whatever damage she'd sustained, her nanobots would be working to fix. Like most cyborgs, she'd gained tougher skin over a stronger skeletal structure resulting in enhanced strength as well as increased visual, auditory and olfactory upgrades to her sensory levels.

But right now, she struggled to regain control of herself. It was a testament to how weak she must be to let those outside her pod view her like this. While their transition to elite soldiers managed to keep a lot of their organics, the rest of their bodies had been turned into powerhouse machines with high-level capabilities thanks to the cybernetics.

Along with some other unexpected side effect benefits. Sora eliminating the shield was a potential indication of such a side effect. Unless the rest of them could do it and had never considered such? Cyllus stored the question for later.

"What are you looking at? Let's go," she snapped.

"Are you functional?" Cyllus made himself ask. He had no care for her, she was an unknown and possible threat but courtesy had been a gift from his mother that cybernetics couldn't fully eliminate.

"Fine," she grunted.

The answer was good enough. They rushed through the doorway, Sora in the lead, Cyllus behind her and the others right on his heels. Silence settled like an ominous eerie whisper in the halls. Even as he searched for guards, Cyllus left his neural net open to transmit everything to Xion and Kaito. Kelix did the same, their images overlapping.

Their escape from the cells was being shared with the other cyborgs. Sora to her pod and Reo and Tagan to their respective pods. Word rapidly spread and Cyllus knew their actions motivated the others. Shields dropped all around. Thunderous booms signaled that more and more cyborgs had somehow figured out a way to break through their cells.

Soon the hall resonated with the sound of boots pounding. Had to be guards. Cyborgs could be silent when they chose and no greater time called for stealth than now.

They managed to reach the end of their hall when it happened. Alarms blared and emergency lights lined in the ceiling flashed bright red. Communication with his pod flew back and forth.

"Kaito and I are out," Xion muttered.

"How long before the explosives go off?" Kelix asked.

None of them knew.

Up ahead, guards shouted. Uniformed crew members yelled and joined the guards in making a dash toward the lower levels.

"They're heading for the escape shuttles and emergency units," Sora informed them.

"Evac! All personnel evac immediately. The prisoners must not get free!"

The voice on the intercom system was frantic. The guards had realized the prisoners were loose. Warnings and alerts continued to go off, any attempt at secrecy thrown to the wayside as announcements warned of the cyborgs breaking out and attempting to flee.

More than likely, if Shui followed on his current pattern of behavior, there would be limited vessels to use for escape. Enough for the guards and crew to get back to Kirs. Surely not enough for those labeled rebels who weren't expected to survive.

"We have to get to the bay and get off this ship," Tagan announced, drawing to a halt as the confusion in the hall grew and the crowds of cyborgs fighting guards increased.

Cyllus suppressed his growing worry. Calm settled in his core. Whatever happened here would be happening on each of the transports bound for Tyurma in some form or another, including the one with his mother and sister. They didn't have him or the members of his pod to protect them.

"You! Get back in your cell!"

Cyllus ducked the fist flying toward his face and pivoted. He gripped his assailant's wrist, inches from his jaw, turned the arm and snapped the bone. The guard howled and dropped to one knee, holding his injured arm.

There was no remorse in Cyllus for his action. The guards were as guilty as Shui in his mind. They knew what was in store for them and had no qualms about sending innocents to their death.

Ignoring the pained whimpers, Cyllus nodded at Kelix. "Let's go. Xion and Kaito are on the move too."

If possible, they'd try to reconnect with their pod mates. Punching and shoving, Cyllus made his way to the nearest lift registered on his internal scanners.

"Stop!" Someone gripped his shoulder and spun Cyllus around.

He leaned into the movement, hooked an arm about the guard's neck and tugged. The guard jolted then slumped in his arms. Cyllus dropped the dead man and jumped over the body. Tagan, Kelix, Sora and Reo were just as brutal, slaying everyone who got in their way.

It was good that he could shut down his emotions. Killing never sat well with him. This was an exception. Their escape had become a life or death fight. Cyllus blocked out the cries, the blood and the crack of limbs as he fought each guard or crew member trying to stop him. Cold. He had to stay cold.

Ahead, he recognized the area for the lift and slowed. The door access buzzed when he touched the vid screen, denying them entry. Cyllus drove his fist into the panel with a fierce punch and the doors slid open. The others crowded in with him.

"Your internal processor couldn't bypass the security?" Reo asked with a smirk as he leaned against the opposite wall with his arms crossed over his broad chest.

Cyllus ignored him, shoving away the fear working through his systems. It had been rash, but he didn't care when expediency was needed. No amount of emotion suppression was helping to block off thoughts of his mother and sister. His biggest concern right now was getting off this ship alive and saving his family.

By any means necessary.

Chapter 2

"Where are you two? Kaito and I are in the departure bay. We managed to identify an available ship on the east side section of the bay. Soon others will try to overrun us and take it for themselves," Xion reported.

The lift stopped on each floor and more cyborgs forced their way in. All had the same hope. To get off the transport and survive.

On one floor, the doors opened to four guards standing on the other side. Their eyes widened at the sight of the massive cyborgs crowded on the lift and the click of stolen weapons aimed directly at them.

"Run!" one of them screamed, already turning on his heels in the other direction.

The doors shut moments later.

"I'm not sure how long it will take us to arrive." The transport ships were huge and there were several levels to go on this particular fleet design before they reached the cargo and launch bay areas. *"Leave. Kelix and I will manage and rendezvous with you and Kaito as soon as possible."*

The quiet contemplation over their NNP lasted less than ten point fifty three seconds.

"Agreed," Xion said.

"Agreed," Kaito chimed in.

Across the lift, Kelix sent Cyllus a sharp nod. They'd work together and fight to join their brethren, but right now, they had to focus on each of them getting out. If that meant separating, then so be it. Survival was the most important thing at this point.

Finally, they reached the last level at the bottom of the transport. Exiting the lift, Cyllus walked into a bay area in the midst of pure chaos. The constant whoosh and glide of ships fleeing the doomed transport acted as a constant hum in the background.

Kelix came to stand beside him. "It won't be long before there are no means of escape. We'll go down with this transport if we don't move immediately."

Unacceptable. Cyllus had to rescue the only family he had left.

Sora eased up on Cyllus' other side. "My pod shared they managed to escape their transport in a short-range shuttle."

That was all she said. Nothing else. Cyllus eyed Tagan and the gruff cyborg's upper lip curled in a snarl before he snapped, "My pod is out of range and I'm unable to contact them. I must work under the assumption they have fled their transport as well."

His crystalline green eyes flickered with concern, then his shoulders straightened and he met Cyllus' gaze head on, flares of fiery anger at their circumstances easy to read.

Reo spoke next. "The members of my pod are on another transport as well. Its' become obvious that each of us was deliberately separated and placed with cyborgs we have no connection with when possible. We have very little choice in our next moves. It's in our best interest to work together."

Cyllus' sneered at the emperor's cunning. Reo was right. Separating them from their individual pods meant they were forced to rely on one another. Virtual unknowns they had no connection to outside their joint service in the Military Elite.

Running probability checks came up with the same results. There was no choice. "That's the best solution in this circumstance. We go together and figure out the next steps after we're free."

Their conversation hadn't taken long but it was clear there were fewer vessels remaining than when they'd stepped out of the lift.

Continued screams and pleas could be heard from the civilians, guards and crew being left behind. Some cyborgs were doing their best to herd them to safety in available ships while others took the logical approach and saved themselves. The latter were wise. More chance of success.

Even as the thought crossed his mind, Cyllus cringed. His mother and sister would be viewed as the same disadvantage. Would someone see to their escape?

He must have made a sound of distress because Kelix jerked toward him and arched a brow. Cyllus sent a reassuring nod his way and composed himself. It was one of the few flaws in his programming.

The organic side of him fought to retain a strong connection to his blooded family. He couldn't always be cold and ruthless about their existence the way his machine half demanded. Like now.

Chances of escape dropped with each second they delayed. Cyllus ran to join the fray. "Hurry!"

Bypassing the individual escape pods and smaller ships, their group drew to a stop near a larger shuttle. This wasn't for simple emergency evacuations. This was something the crew used for surface missions if needed or long distance transport.

"Who can pilot this?" Sora asked, a deep frown pulling her dark brows into a v. "I don't have schematics stored for flying."

"I do." Kelix placed his hand on the panel of the shuttle's door.

It slid open and they all charged inside the ramp that led straight into the interior. They stopped at the closed door of the bridge.

"I've taken control of the onboard computers and all electronics," Kelix muttered, gaining entry.

Their cells may have been designed to block cyborgs from hacking or overriding but everything else on the transport was vulnerable to cyborg manipulation, including these ships.

Cyllus dropped into one of the navigation seats. Tagan took a seat at an armory station alongside Sora. At least this vessel had basic weapon capabilities. That was something he was sure they'd need. Reo filed in last and strapped in behind Cyllus.

While Kelix manned the helm, alerts continued to blare from outside the shuttle. His friend narrowed his gaze and aimed the vessel for the bay doors that opened and closed in a non-stop motion. Ships and shuttles launched in a steady stream into the blackness of space.

According to the scanners Cyllus accessed and the display tablet in front of him, individual pods, smaller shuttles, and a few carrier ships surged from the underbelly of the transport like rapid bursts from a laser as everyone raced away. Escape and timing was of the essence.

"This will be a bit rough," Kelix warned.

The ship rumbled as it started then smoothed out. They turned unerringly toward the open bay doors. Cyllus double-checked his harness then plotted the course for the nearest station. It was several days away but would have to do. They couldn't return to Kirs until they had a chance to figure out Shui's plan and how to defeat him.

As they neared the doors, the two-seater ship to their left shot forward nearly clipping them. Kelix cursed, adjusted for the near miss, yet continued to accelerate. At their current pace, they should have sufficient speed to clear the transport. Hopefully before the explosives.

"Any update on when the bombs were set to go off?" Reo asked in his deep gravelly voice.

"I'm not open to the mainframe," Tagan said, lips twisted in a grim smile. "For obvious reasons."

Right. They couldn't trust the public internal means cyborgs generally used to communicate with one another now that the emperor had proven he could hack his way into those databases. Only the neural net they shared with their individual pods was truly private and Cyllus for damn sure wasn't inviting anyone else into his personal core.

"Almost there," Sora muttered under her breath.

The concentration on her face was solid. He'd expect no less from a fellow cyborg. Cyllus checked Kelix to see he handled the ship with ease, no visible tension in the fluid lines of his body. If there was anyone Cyllus trusted to get them through this, it was Kelix. His best friend had a knack for landing on his feet in any scenario. The trust they had in one another went both ways.

"Oh, fuck! Hurry!" Tagan shouted.

Curses from the others followed. Cyllus checked the navigation display and didn't see anything of note. He ran a scan with the onboard computer and discovered what the others already had. Fire.

Fed by the oxygen inside, flames crawled up the interior walls of the bay. Remaining ships burst into balls of orange and blue one after the other. Fleeing people were caught in the raging inferno. Cyllus turned from the sight. Their screams would live in his nightmares.

Survive. He just had to survive. That was all that mattered. The ship's overdrive kicked in, the pressure pinning Cyllus to his seat. He gripped his armrests and left everything in the hands of fate.

Their shuttle launched through the opening just in time. Behind them, the concussion of the exploding transport shook and rocked their shuttle.

"Shields holding," Sora said into the quiet.

Cyllus blew out a soft breath. He didn't want to think of the lives lost—those who didn't make it in time.

"I can't reach Xion and Kaito."

Kelix communicated to Cyllus on their NNP. Cyllus reached out to the other two men who were like brothers to him. Silence. Not the empty hole of death he'd heard other cyborgs refer to when trying to describe the sensation of losing pod members.

"Perhaps the distance is too great."

"Likely."

It was more than likely. Xion and Kaito left before them. It stood to reason they had enough time to travel farther in their escape. Cyllus wouldn't have expected otherwise. They could rendezvous later.

"We'll find them," Cyllus said with confidence. His mother and sister too.

He had to believe that.

Chapter 3

With regret and remorse filling her soul, Savie said goodbye to the last companion from the science development research team. She closed the lid on the bio unit, blocking Alain's still face from view.

His upright tube was one of eleven with the green occupied light blinking. At the end of the row the twelfth container remained empty. Waiting.

In the corner beside it, a plaque read S. Monroe. For her when she eventually died like the others.

Two weeks had gone by, and it was official. She, the human woman formerly of Earth known as Savannah Monroe, was going to die. She didn't want to think that way but the other workers in the exploratory science lab who had arrived here were all gone.

Alain had dragged himself back from outside, bleeding severely from gashes all over. His clothes were torn from the strange beasts outside circling the safety dome set up for their research.

He'd assured Savie that going out to reconnect the transceivers and burying them was critical to them being rescued. The beacon would set off a continuous alert to make any ship in the vicinity aware of their need for help.

Arguing that the creatures would tear him apart hadn't stopped him from leaving.

"We have to, Savie. Otherwise, we're as dead as the others," Alain said, referencing their team members.

Now he was dead. The venom had worked quickly and he hadn't suffered more than necessary as Savie injected him with sedative after sedative to keep the pain to a minimum as much as possible.

She was the last survivor.

The thought had her stomach churning. Or that could be hunger. Lack of food, worry and fear left her in a confused state. One in which she vacillated between thinking today was her last day, then holding hope someone would answer the emergency beacon and she'd be rescued.

Of the twelve workers from Earth selected for this ill-fated trip, Savie was the last.

The last.

She couldn't shake that fact. Two on the science team had died when they tried to flee to the ship they'd arrived on only to discover the Elusans hadn't left the vessel behind for them. The others had succumbed to the wild animals that invaded the domed science station they'd set up two months ago.

Slumping to the floor, Savie sighed and leaned her head back against the cabinet behind her. Her gaze traveled warily around the lab where she'd cornered herself for safety. Steel doors that could only be locked from the inside protected her. For now.

Why had she agreed to this trip? She was a botanist. A plant specialist. Yet the idea of being a part of a team sent to travel the stars for the first time, to be on an unknown world and experience space travel had been too good to pass up. Sighing again, she dropped her chin to her chest and picked at a loose thread on her one-piece beige flight suit.

So much had happened in such a short period of time. Zombies on Earth, the Vassi aliens arriving in time with a cure, then the other alien race, the Elusans, making a secret offer to Lexie. The Elusans were the ones who'd followed the Vassi to Earth and worked out the deal to send a small research team to this world.

Savie sniffed and banged her fist on the tiled floor. "Fuckers!"

Shoving up to her feet, she wobbled as a wave of dizziness rolled over her. Once she regained her balance, she crossed the space to the lone desk against the wall and sat in the chair. It contoured to her body, providing maximum comfort. Savie took no pleasure in the technology unlike the first time she'd experienced it.

Marveling at the wonders the Elusans provided had lost its luster when she realized they'd dropped her team off on a vacant landscape with deadly wildlife and poisonous plants. Then vanished.

Initially, their team of twelve hadn't cared. They were too fascinated with being on an alien world and given the chance to explore.

If they had waited or gone through official government channels, there was a strong chance none of them would have been selected for a mission like this for months. Years even. Once Earth joined the Protectorate, an alliance of distant worlds, the Vassi had designated themselves as mentors and took the role seriously.

It was hard to imagine aliens existed. It was rumored, laughed about but not given serious consideration after centuries of no contact.

Now Savie was trapped on an undeveloped planet. Alone. After Jake and Kara died, the rest of them had been afraid to contact Earth or the Protectorate due to their unapproved deal with the Elusans.

Hell.

Savie stabbed at the crystal like screen until it opened on the recording she'd left incomplete yesterday. This was her audio journal and cry for help at the same time. Savie cleared her throat and keyed the mic. "It's me again. Day fourteen. I'm not sure at this point if anyone will hear these messages. I think...I think no one is coming. I won't be rescued before the supplies run out."

She swallowed and her shoulders sagged. Saying the truth aloud made it more real. Her food and purified water rations were low. Maybe a few more days. Two weeks at the most if she stretched it. How long could she live after the food and water were gone?

She tapped the mic again. "Anyway, I'm leaving this record behind so someone knows I existed. I was someone."

Savie blinked back tears and continued. "Back on Earth I have a dad, cousins and friends. They didn't want me to come on this trip. I ignored their warnings. Twenty-six and all-knowing, right?"

Her laugh held a bitter edge but Savie couldn't do anything about that. "The rest of my entries will be about me and not the crew or what we were doing here on Algor 1."

That was the name they'd voted to give this deadly world. Oh, the hopes and dreams they'd all had with being the first to leave Earth. The secrecy of it all made the situation even more enticing.

Fools. They'd been fools to believe strange aliens with glowing forms and telepathic voices had their best interest at heart. It was becoming more and more clear that the Elusans only wanted to establish a relationship on Earth without the Protectorates' knowledge. Why, she didn't know and at this point, Savie didn't care.

Clearing her throat, she said, "My favorite color is blue. I like fruit. All kinds. Doesn't matter what it is. I prefer rainy days to sunny days. Rain makes it feel like there's a fresh new start. That fills me with joy. To know that when it rains every thing gets a fresh chance to start anew."

***

"My favorite color is blue. I like fruit. All kinds. Doesn't matter what it is. I prefer rainy days to sunny days. Rain makes it feel like there's a fresh new start. That fills me with joy. To know that when it rains everything gets a fresh chance to start anew."

Cyllus listened to the soft feminine voice wisping along his auditory circuits. Stretched out on his narrow bed in the room he'd claimed as his on the stolen ship, Cyllus felt the stiff restraints around his heart softening.

It was hard to stay disconnected with the female's words ringing in his ear. He'd caught the transmissions accidentally during a routine scan with the ship's systems to find a safe port for them and hopefully track down Xion and Kaito.

During those checks, Cyllus also discovered that the emperor's public warnings regarding anyone with a facial branding had spread far and wide. They'd been labeled traitors.

This female had broadcast recordings along a path reserved for emergency signals. Kelix caught the alert next when he'd relieved Cyllus of duty watch and voted to ignore it.

By logic, it had been three weeks since this message was recorded and the individual had probably already succumbed to death. They couldn't afford to endanger their safety by responding to a rescue request on an unidentified dwarf planet that wasn't supposed to be occupied by anything other than the native wildlife anyway.

The others agreed and Cyllus bowed to the inevitable despite wanting to investigate. He had to be rational. The woman meant nothing and a useless stop served no purpose. They were right. She was more than likely dead anyway

As they traveled closer and closer to AB476, as it was listed on the navigational maps, Cyllus resumed the audio messages. Journal entries she called them. He'd played all of them in the hours since the vote to keep traveling. Her voice wrapped around him and filled Cyllus with an emotion he couldn't explain.

Every cell, organic and cybernetic, clung to the sensation. It helped him block the pain and agony of not knowing if his mother and sister were alive or dead. Her voice soothed even as it riled an unclaimed part of him and broke through the cold reserve he needed to maintain his sanity.

Rolling onto his back on his bunk, Cyllus braced one hand under his head and scrolled back to listen to the recordings again, sorted by his favorite then the ones where her tone carried the most emotion. He paused on the one which stirred his own similar feelings of guilt.

"I did a bad thing and it's why I'm here. Stranded on a dangerous world. Aliens known as the Vassi have been kind and caring to us on Earth. It's unclear how contact was established but they are cautious as to which humans get to leave Earth. Lots of protocol and rules for clearance. Travel to Earth from other worlds is banned without clearance from the Protectorate."

A pause. Deep sigh.

"I didn't understand all of the strict rules. I thought it was crazy and unfair. I get it now. Not all aliens have good intentions." A sniffle. The sound tugged at long dormant heartstrings in his chest. *"I didn't tell my family the truth. The Vassi didn't invite me for an exploratory trip. It was the Elusans who arrived on Earth in secret. The Elusans who put together a team claiming it was a sincere endeavor."*

The Elusans were a long lived race. Powerful and so far advanced and beyond many beings that they no longer took corporal form. Their homeworld was long gone and they'd once roamed among the stars for enlightenment before disappearing.

Cyllus couldn't figure out why this planet, Earth, she spoke of would have drawn the attention of the Elusans. According to...Savie, they were not as developed and didn't have space travel capabilities. Nothing about that should have drawn the interest of such high level beings.

His processors dinged mid-thought. Cyllus froze. That was the alert he'd tagged on the ship for the female from Earth. He sat up straight. It was a journal entry. How? He'd checked and rechecked that he'd downloaded all of the recordings.

Quickly accessing the onboard computer and scanning for incoming data, he noted this recording was new and not one of the ones he'd repeatedly listened to.

"Day 51. Please. Food ran out and I drank the last of the preserved water two days ago. If anyone is out there, if anyone hears this message, I beg you to save me. I...I don't want to die like this."

It was the same female though her voice didn't carry the melodic notes of her earlier messages. None of the calm and poise as she accepted the inevitable. No humor as she recounted the lighter aspects of her experience. In this one, her voice cracked and husked with desperation and terror hung on each word.

The time and date were less than five minutes ago. She was still alive! Another scan and he confirmed their ship was mere hours away from her. Even as the thought registered, Cyllus slammed his feet into his boots and reached out to Kelix. *"The woman on AB476 is alive."*

"She is of no import, Cyllus."

Cyllus forced his fingers to unclench and raced out of his room into the corridor that led to the bridge. Sora might be with Kelix on the bridge but the others would be in their own quarters taking a designated break as Cyllus had been doing.

He reached the bridge and slid sideways through the door as soon as it began to open. Kelix spun in his chair and met his gaze. Calm radiated from his black eyes as he watched Cyllus' stormy approach. Sora glanced up from the navigational panel, frowned then turned back to her station without more of a reaction.

The others tended to ignore him and Kelix when they butted heads. Being from the same pod, their closeness was expected and accepted, along with their sometimes volatile disagreements. Cyllus had once been the leader of their pod and his nature demanded he resume the role.

Never again, though. As Cyllus drew close to his friend, he battled those urges to let Kelix take charge. He didn't want to make decisions ever again that put lives at risk. It was better to keep his emotions in the cold place. Until now.

Kelix held his hand up before Cyllus could speak. "There are bounties on our head, Cyllus. This could be a trap."

Cyllus breathed out softly. He'd considered that. They were far enough from Kirs but not far enough from the emperor's reach if he wanted to recapture the cyborgs who'd fled.

Still. The woman was from an unknown planet. Stuck on a strange world. "The Elusans doomed their group to die there."

"According to her," Kelix countered, settling back in his chair. He folded his hands over his midsection and tipped his head to the side. "Think on it, Cy. We've never heard of this Earth she mentions. There are less than a dozen Elusans known to still be in existence. At their advanced state of evolution, why would they lower themselves to bother with a race lacking in the technology many of us take for granted?"

Kelix was right but Cyllus kept hearing her voice in his head. *Please. I don't want to die.* How could he ignore such a plea? "We're soldiers, Kelix. Tasked with helping those in need."

Jerking upright, Kelix dropped his feigned nonchalance and thrust a finger at the floor. "We're outlaws. Criminals on the run for war crimes and anything else Shui wants to charge us with. Our task, as you put it, is to survive and find Kaito and Xion."

Sora made a noise under her breath and Kelix spared her a glance. "Find *all* of our pod brethren. We don't have the time to put ourselves in danger for someone we don't know."

Truth. Truth. Truth. Everything Kelix said was true. Her story didn't make sense. Cyllus bowed his head, prepared to accept the inevitable and make the right decision. He must walk away from the strange female's plight.

Ding.

A new alert. Another journal entry. Cyllus sent his mind into the ship's computer banks to listen.

"I'm going to die. I think...I think I should make peace with that. No one's coming. The food stores ran out. I finished the last bottle of water. Two days ago? I can't remember. I'm not at peace, though. I had dreams." Her voice rose on the last statement. Defiance and anger rolled into one. "I wanted a husband and children. I wanted laughter and joy. It's not fair that my desire to see beyond my world should end like this."

Cyllus raised his head and met Kelix's stern gaze. He'd caught that last transmission as well. Probably locked on to the signal once Cyllus barged in. Sora turned sideways in her chair. She, too, had probably heard the woman's words. With her lips pressed into a thin line, she arched a brow and waited to see what their next move would be.

Sora was as hard and cold as any male cyborg Cyllus had worked with. While the numbers of female cyborgs didn't come close to the males, he'd met a few and Sora would rank at the top of individuals he didn't want to cross. Male or female.

In their limited time together, she'd been forced to knock Reo out with one punch after a particularly ugly argument. It was during one of the other cyborg's spiraling moments whenever he reflected on losing his pod mates.

That bit of news had devastated all of them. In a blink, Reo's entire pod was wiped from his NNP.

Sora's actions had won Tagan over with her aggressive nature. Tagan lived to fight and create havoc for the sake of being contrary. How he'd managed to be a decorated soldier in their military, Cyllus had yet to figure out.

The feminine voice burst into his mind again as she began to speak, her journal entries live instead of dated because Cyllus hadn't unlinked from the ship's system.

"Trusting the Elusans was a big mistake."

Something in the way she said the last caused Cyllus' gut to tighten. It was hard to remain cold in the face of her fear and uncertainty. "We're going to rescue her."

Kelix narrowed his eyes but didn't counter his order. Sora adjusted in her seat, fingers flying. The ship was too well built to actually feel the directional change but it was nothing for Cyllus to reach out with his processors and see the new coordinates entered. They were going to AB476. To save Savie.

It could also be the site of their downfall if Cyllus had miscalculated her sincerity. He met Kelix's gaze and saw the same resolve. Kelix expected this to be a trap and still didn't countermand Cyllus. If they were to die, they'd die together.

Because there was no way they could let Shui capture them and tear into their neural net processors. If the emperor managed to break into their NNP, he could destroy the remaining hidden rebels.

Chapter 4

Savie blew out a breath and flicked the switch to turn off the recorder. No more journal entries. That was her last one. The counter showed she'd recorded thirty-eight additional messages since her arrival on Algor 1. Most were from the last three weeks as she pleaded for rescue.

A smile twisted her lips as she sighed and slid down the backside of the desk to sit on her butt. Wishing and hoping had proven to be wasteful.

Legs sprawled before her, realization set in. No one was coming. Her team had been dumped in a no man's land. Her brain circled around the idea the Elusans had done this on purpose. Savie still couldn't imagine why, but it didn't change the facts.

Gazing around at the lab with its discarded soil samples and potted greenery, her heart stuttered. She'd put so much effort into her initial work here only for things to end this way.

Quiet reigned outside. She tapped on a screen for the few active interior cams and her throat locked. The creatures had increased in numbers. *Jobas.* They'd named them when they first arrived and caught sight of the striped feline like animals with short forearms and large haunches. Their tails whipped about, the spikes on the end emitting a deadly poison on contact.

Savie shoved a hand through her tumbled hair. They'd learned about the poison the hard way. Darius, the lead scientist in the group, had been testing samples on the grounds outside their dome when a *joba* surprised him.

He'd made it back inside after being struck twice on the back with the appendage. Because the air here was compatible with their needs, though thin, he hadn't had on a bio suit or any protective gear. Just his shirt and pants paired with sturdy boots.

Lexie, the medic assigned on the trip, hadn't thought the small punctures on his back to be too much of a danger. She'd cleaned them, bandaged him and given Darius an all inclusive antibiotic. Everyone had a good laugh over the incident at lunch a few hours later recounting the event.

Darius' sharp brown features creased in a wide grin as he explained coming face to face with the *joba*. "I think we scared each other. I jumped up and hauled ass but it was right on my heels. Whipped me twice with that long tail. Stung like a bitch at the time. Now I don't feel anything."

"We need to be more careful of the wildlife here," Lexie warned though her eyes glinted with humor.

"Man, I thought you'd fall for sure." Stefan stood up and ran in a circle, pretending to be Darius.

Sweet, kind Stefan who brought to the team his expertise in the study of microbiology.

Chuckling, Darius tossed his balled napkin at Stefan. "I'd like to see you outrun it."

More laughter from the team followed because Stefan, for all his six-foot height and long gangly legs, was about as unathletic as you could get. A proud nerd with no aspirations to physical strength he'd loudly proclaimed often.

"At least you looked smooth. Hair didn't budge," Alain teased.

Darius flexed and ran a hand over his smooth haircut, which he often bragged about doing himself.

"Hopefully, none of us have to—" Savie was adding her own comment when Darius reached for his throat and gagged. "Dare, what's wrong?"

He lurched to his feet, tugging at his collar, eyes wide and stumbling against his chair. Lexie jumped up and was by his side in an instant. One hand braced on his back and the other trying to put her sensor on his forehead for a reading. "Darius! Darius!"

He fell backward, knocking over the dishes from the meal and hit the floor, choking and gurgling. All of them scrambled to their feet. Savie's heart pounded with fear. She dropped to her knees and clutched his flailing hand. His fingers locked tight to hers and his head tipped to the side to see her.

"I'm here, Darius. Right here with you," she said.

His brown skin grew pallid while white film lined the sides of his lips. He continued to arch and struggle, the sounds coming from his throat raising the hair on her arms. Blinking back tears, Savie faced Lexie. "What's wrong with him?"

The medic worked quickly and efficiently, her opened pack at her side as she injected Darius. She eventually stabilized him. His eyes drifted close and his body went lax.

"Holy fuck," Stefan gasped.

Murmurs flowed from the others. Confusion and fear glinted in their concerned gazes. They managed to carry Darius to the small clinic where Lexie could run full tests to see what caused his fit. Outwardly he appeared fine, no traces of harm.

Day after day, it became more obvious that something serious had befallen Darius. They visited in cycles, hope and pleas for his recovery on everyone's lips whenever they talked and tried to figure out what exactly had happened. He'd been laughing only moments before collapsing.

Unfortunately, Darius never woke again, fading gradually until his heart stopped on the fifth day of his coma like state. Blood results came back with toxic levels of poison in his body. He was dead the moment the *joba's* tail lashed him. He just didn't know it.

Savie shook away the memory. Darius had been the first to die. Then the others. One by one until it had only been her, Alain and Stefan left. The *jobas* weren't simple animals. They were intelligent, malevolent beings.

Their attacks mirrored a well-choreographed plan. They circled the dome day and night, keeping them from being able to leave. The security alerts around the perimeter as well as the vid cams were knocked down one after the other.

In a short amount of time, the *jobas* had gotten inside the dome. First, only one or two of the creatures. Then the numbers grew and soon they spread throughout the facility.

Lexie decided that being in one space would be safer. She advised moving to one location. Everyone grabbed what they could and moved to the central lab, fighting and dodging the *jobas* to do that.

In a panic, Patel and Himari fled to the area for the ship that brought them here. It wasn't there and the *jobas* took them down before anyone could help get them back in the dome. Snacks kept in the cold storage ran out quickly. Kara and Lexie risked themselves to grab more food to stock in the lab. They hadn't made it back.

Maurice, Claire and Toby had fallen in an ill-fated race back to the safety of the lab after going to retrieve Kara's and Lexie's bodies. The *jobas* tore them apart.

After that, Alain, Stefan and Savie knew they were trapped unless they could get the satellite security relays and transceiver back up. Their hope had been to connect with the Elusans and explain what happened. Beg to be taken back to Earth.

Stefan volunteered to go. It wasn't hard to see the pure terror on his face as he made the offer. He carried a large broken leg from one of the tables for protection. Alain and Savie waited with baited breath to see if he'd be successful. Right after the signal came online, Savie heard Stefan scream in the halls on his return trip back inside.

"Lock the doors of the lab, Savie! Don't come out here," Stefan yelled.

She'd run to do what he said. Slamming her palms on the steel doors and securing them, she'd sobbed at his screams and cries of pain. It seemed to go on forever until the silence.

Silence followed by the hollow click clack of claws on tile. Then scratching on the door she leaned against. Scratches and growls. Alain had sobbed beside her. He and Stefan had been friends since their university days.

It was a defining moment. The bleak look on Alain's face told Savie he'd given up hope with Stefan's death.

Alain's last act to reconnect the communication device and bury it under a mound of rocks to keep the *jobas* from taking it down again had been sacrificial in nature but he must have known what would happen.

Days turned to weeks. Weeks she'd been alone and hopeful for rescue. But now...

Shoving to her feet, Savie wobbled then braced a hand on the desk to catch her balance. Lack of food and water messed with her awareness. If Lexie were still alive she'd be pushing a protein stick in Savie's hand.

But Lexie was gone and there were no more protein sticks. Savie had eaten them all. Unable to forage for food or reach the other sections of the dome due to the number of *jobas* taking up residence inside left her little choice but to starve.

Occasionally she heard the knicker and whine of the creatures pacing outside the door. Sometimes they slammed their bodies against it, trying to force their way inside. At other times, she heard moans and cries.

This time she swore the noise sounded like a baby and Savie panicked, thinking someone else was stuck here with her beyond the doors. Someone with a baby. Going to the door, her hand on the lock, she was close to opening it when the familiar growl and rumble replaced the cries.

Either the *jobas* were excellent mimics, or the hallucinations had started. Savie leaned toward the latter. Hallucinations she knew would be the end of her

*****

Armored and geared up, Cyllus faced Tagan. The other cyborg was a war machine in his own right. Discovering they intended to land to rescue an unknown female had not been met with pleasure.

After listening to a handful of the new recordings, Tagan changed his mind without further explanation.

"We've detected native wildlife around the perimeter of the structure where the female vital signs are being registered," Tagan said.

Savie was alive. For now. It had taken three hours to reach the dwarf planet. Vast masses of water covered most of AB476, but dry surface areas teemed with organic life forms. Mostly land-dwelling animals.

Focusing on the emergency beacon led them directly to a large dome structure. Not as sophisticated as what Kirsians used when scouting or setting up bio locations in unchartered countries on their world but it seemed basic enough.

According to the ship's long range scanner, only one humanoid presence was detected. It showed as a fiery red and orange blob located at the center of the dome.

Dozens of creatures surrounded the facility with a few more detected in the interior. Their cooler body temps reflected as yellow and green circles. Cyllus counted over two dozen on the outside of the dome alone. That was their main concern once they landed.

"We're unsure if the wildlife is aggressive, so stay on guard." This from Tagan. He may have been initially disgruntled at their decision but once engaged, his input was nothing less than professional and invaluable.

Reo hovered at the door. Cyllus didn't expect him to speak, but the other cyborg's gaze held steely resolve.

Cyllus rechecked his weapons. Two lasers, four sonic grenades and power cells for recharging the guns. "How long?"

"We can give you two hours," Kelix answered. "After that, we need to leave. No matter what."

He emphasized the last point with a glare in Cyllus' direction. Two hours. Sora had caught what they thought might be another ship approaching at rapid speed. It would arrive shortly and either pass along or discover their presence and investigate.

They didn't need the attention.

"I'll be back in time, but if not, leave." The words were a lie. Cyllus had no intentions of returning to their ship without Savie. He couldn't explain it and only hoped he wouldn't be bringing back a body.

Sora handed him a clear face mask to enable him to breathe and a spare for Savie which he added to the light pack on his back. The air was thin and supported life, but they weren't taking any chances. Plus, it would help if Cyllus had to deal with any toxic gases inside the domed facility.

"Alright. I'm heading out." Cyllus turned and hit the button to lower the ramp. Steps eager, he charged down while it was still in motion.

From behind him, Kelix called out, "Two hours, Cy!"

He raised his hand in acknowledgment but didn't turn back. Kelix had decided not to land too close to the dome structure in case the female's recordings were indeed a setup to draw them in. The distance meant Cyllus would have to run there to save time. There was no way the woman from Earth would be able to match his speed on the return trip back. Not to mention he might be carrying a dead body back.

No. Savannah Monroe had to be alive.

Cyllus raced in the direction his sensors indicated. There was no way to communicate his presence to her or that the rescue she pleaded for was within reach. Her journal entries were public without a reply function and the emergency alert was a simple signal that negated a response system.

None of that mattered if he arrived in time. Cyllus just needed her to hang on a little longer.

I'm coming, Savie. Don't give up yet.

Chapter 5

"Savannah Monroe."

Savie jerked awake at the sound of her name being called.

"Savannah Monroe, are you here?"

Blinking, Savie shoved into an upright position. She glanced around and realized she was on the floor. Her hair fell about her face in lank sweaty sections. Groaning, she shoved it behind her ear.

"Savannah Monroe!"

Who called for her? Savie stood and stared around in dazed confusion. "Stefan? Alain?"

Were they alive?

Her heart thumped in excited response. The white walls of the lab spun around her. "Darius? Lexie, is that you?"

Savie glanced at the row of bio units lined against the wall in shadow. The interiors were dark due to the preservation system set to run on minimum power.

Maybe they'd survived after all! Spinning around in excitement, Savie ignored the containment tubes and raced to the locked steel door. The barrier was the only thing that stood between her and her friends. As soon as she reached it, she heard the sounds.

Growls. In an instant, her memory flooded back. Her friends and teammates were dead. Letting her forehead hit the door, Savie sniffed as a single tear tracked down her cheek. It wasn't Alain, Stefan, Darius or Lexie.

Just *jobas*. The creatures which had trapped them here and taken them out one by one.

The growls suddenly broke off, replaced by frantic yelps. Savie frowned and stood back. The camera in the outer hall had been damaged, giving her a limited view of the other side. It still worked because it was too high for the animals to reach and completely destroy.

Savie went to the mounted screen and flicked the touchpad to activate it. Her gasp filled the air. Backs hunched and lips curled in a snarl to reveal rows of sharp teeth, the *jobas* out there started edging away from a section in the hallway.

Something else had entered the hall. Something more terrifying. Enough to scare even those wild animals.

Chest tightening with each rasping breath she took, Savie backed away but couldn't drag her gaze from the screen. Another yelp, and the *joba* at the far end of the hall dropped to the ground. Three others took off running in the opposite direction.

Was she dreaming? Savie pressed a hand to her chest. She was fully aware that cognitive issues were a sign of her declining condition. But what if the *jobas* were chased away? She could leave the lab she'd been entombed in. Maybe find food and water.

The thought alone was enough to spur her hope. Her stomach rumbled in agreement.

Throat dry, Savie couldn't break her gaze away from the screen and the now empty corridor. Then fear returned in a flash. If the *jobas* ran from something more dangerous, it couldn't be good for Savie. Anything that frightened those predators would surely rip her to pieces.

Pounding on the door accompanied another shout. She jumped and faced the door of steel in trepidation.

"Savannah Monroe! Are you alright?"

A male voice. A male who knew her name. Excitement replaced the fear and she took a step toward the door to release the locks. Her fingers trembled, but before Savie released the last one, reason returned.

How could she be sure this wasn't a hallucination? She glanced at the spot on the floor where she spent most of her days of late, the crumpled blanket familiar. Discarded wrappings from food she'd eaten days ago lay in a pile she'd created. Some of them were folded in her odd version of origami.

This wasn't right. No one was here. The Elusans had left her team over a month ago with promises to return and assist their observations. Lies. Instead they'd been abandoned with no way to return to Earth.

Her hands fell to her side and Savie slumped against the door in dismay. The smart thing to do would be chain herself to a table leg so she didn't open the door and let the *jobas* in to devour her.

"My sensors indicate a live being. If you are Savanna Monroe, I'm here to rescue you."

Rescue. Against her better judgment, she perked up and listened.

"We picked up your beacon. Help has arrived for you."

The voice was deep and male, its even tones soothing and reassuring as he spoke. Alain *had* set the beacons. That was in the before also known as before she'd given up hope. Before when she'd broadcast her journal entries thinking rescue imminent.

"I have less than an hour to return to my ship mates, or they'll leave me. We'll both be stranded, Savannah Monroe, if you don't act soon."

How did he know her name? Or should she accept that as proof this was not real? Her mind could be playing tricks on her, though. Savie slammed a weak fist on the frame and hit the off button for the intercom as she turned away in anger. *Stupid, stupid.* She refused to listen further. Death taunted her with the one thing she wanted.

"Savannah?"

Savie spun around toward the door again. How was he doing this? She'd turned off the intercom. Unless the voice was in her head. She pressed her hands to her ears. "No, no, no."

"Savie?"

She froze. Only her friends and family called her Savie. Battling another surge of hope, Savie dropped her arms. What was real? What was dream and wishful thinking?

"I'm not crazy. I'm not crazy," she muttered under her breath and paced away.

Savie went straight to the locked cabinet against the wall and entered the four-digit code. The door clicked open and labeled sedatives lined the shelves in even rows. Lexie was an organizational queen. Had been. Savie shook as she reached for the injector to put herself to sleep. It was the only way to guarantee she wouldn't open the door and secure her immediate death.

"I'm not leaving without you, Savie." This time the voice projected from the wall speakers.

Maybe she'd created the voice and blocked it from her mind. Did she want to think she was crazy? Panting, Savie gripped the injector between trembling fingers. She needed to knock herself out before she gave in further to her delusions.

"I'm an enhanced cyborg. I've accessed the rudimentary computer systems here," he answered as if he read her mind. "The locking system on this door is more complex. It will take me time we don't have to bypass the biometric lock and backup security. Please open the door."

Holding back whimpers, Savie shook her head in denial though he couldn't see the gesture. It was all a trick by her mind. Once she opened the door, the remaining *jobas* would slaughter her. She rolled up her sleeve and jabbed the injector in her arm.

"I know you didn't think anyone would arrive in time, but I'm *here*, Savie. You're being rescued."

The voice cajoled and Savie found herself walking back toward it, toward the door. She clenched her fists at her sides and licked her cracked lips. Was she about to make the biggest mistake ever? But what did she have to lose? Death waited for her no matter what she did.

Savie watched as if a distant participant. Her fingers shook as she tapped the intercom and turned it back on. "How do I know you're real?"

***

Success! Cyllus held back his shout of triumph. She was alive. Possibly. There was a small margin of chance, less than two percent, that another female resided in the room on the other side of the door he continued to try and hack. He needed clarification. "I'm real. Are you Savanna Monroe?"

"Y-yes. Who are you?"

Cyllus closed his eyes on a sigh. Her voice was rough, hoarse but according to his auditory sensors, it was a ninety-eight percent match for the recordings. This was the woman from Earth. The one who had recorded her innermost thoughts and smashed through his cold exterior to enthrall him.

"My name is Cyllus. Can you open the door?" His cybernetics hit another block as he worked frantically to get through the security protocols in place while maintaining the conversation with her. It was much more detailed than he expected and of higher tech than the outer doors of the facility had been.

"*Hurry, Cy,*" Kelix voice interrupted along their NNP, a constant reminder of his limited time.

Cyllus had killed the animals roaming the halls, but there were more waiting outside they'd have to get through.

"I want to open the door, but I'm afraid," Savie said.

Cyllus curled his fingers against his side of the door and resisted the urge to bang on it in frustration. He took a deep breath and let it out slowly. Calm. He had to remain calm. "I understand your fear. You have to trust me. If you don't come with me, both of us will die."

He was *not* leaving here without her. Especially now that he knew she was alive and so close. So close to him being able to save her. Cyllus needed this more than anything else in years. He *had* to save Savannah Monroe.

"You should leave. The *jobas* will regroup. They travel in packs."

"*Jobas?*" Who else was here with her? He hadn't detected any other signs of life. Or had she meant something else? "The creatures who surround this place?"

"Yes!" she emphasized her answer in a louder voice, much more in line with the sound of the recordings.

One hundred percent match. Cyllus' mouth curled up. She still had fight left in her. She'd need it.

"Forty minutes, Cyllus. Damn it, if you don't have her by now, leave!"

Kelix's annoyed growl was a distraction Cyllus didn't need. He blocked the NNP connection for the first time since they'd awakened as newly minted cyborgs.

Cyllus tried to think of what would convince Savannah Monroe that he was real and not a figment of her imagination. What could he tell her to convince her to open the door while they still had time to escape?

He'd existed in a cold state for so long he barely recalled how to interact with others. Especially women. Giving Savie a ruthless breakdown about their odds and the declining percentage of survival the longer she deterred wouldn't convince her.

Then the answer came to Cyllus.

"My favorite color is blue. I like fruit. All kinds. Doesn't matter what it is. I prefer rainy days to sunny days. Rain makes me feel like there's a fresh new start. That fills me with joy. To know that when it rains every thing gets a fresh chance to start anew."

He felt silly for contemplating it but his actions regarding this woman he didn't know so far were beyond explanation.

Her words had resonated in him from the first time he'd heard them. Now he could only hope she'd spoken in truth.

"My favorite color is black. Not because I like the color but because it hides blood well if there is a battle," Cyllus said.

He picked up her gasp. A sharp, feminine sound. What did she look like? There had been no image files in the journal entries and he hadn't been able to find anything in the ship's database about her world, Earth, let alone the beings who lived there.

"Th—that's different."

Did he detect humor or disgust in her statement? The tremor and raspy nature of her voice distorted any emotion he could read through his senses.

"I don't have a favorite fruit and I like rainy days as well," he added.

Faster than an average mind, Cyllus sorted through her journal entries and picked another. *"Three things about me. I like pizza, I'm a girlie girl sometimes and I love kissing. There's something so intimate and vulnerable about kissing. It tells you a lot about the person."*

Cyllus didn't know what pizza was and only had a vague idea of what she meant by saying she was girlie. The description sounded similar to his sister's traits. He didn't put much stock in kissing but for her, he thought he could like it more.

"Three things about me. I'm a soldier. I'm on the run for crimes I actually committed and...I don't like being vulnerable."

Nothing but the sound of her breathing. Seconds turned to minutes. Time was up. He'd hacked the door two minutes ago but chose not to open it. He'd wanted her trust. Now he'd have to get it another way. Cyllus placed his hand on the door, prepared to open it and grab her before she could run.

The horizontal handle turned in his grip. Stunned, he stepped back. He'd spared the extra time they didn't have in hopes of getting through to her and the gamble had paid off. Pleasure rippled along his senses.

The door slid open and he got his first up and close look at Savannah Monroe from a planet called Earth. Humanoid, bipedal. He hadn't been sure what to expect. Her voice led him to imagine a delicate being, but she was far from that.

Black hair, thick and knotted, tumbled about a face that held remnants of a golden tinge. Her eyes, a brilliant shade of blue, dominated a narrow forehead lined with creases. Sharp cheekbones jutted from a face with visible signs of suffering.

She wore a baggy shirt and pants in a tanned color that did nothing to hide her thin frame. The clothing hung on her shaking form, yet she stood straight and tall, shoulders back.

Savannah Monroe was a survivor. She raised her hand to shove a section of hair behind her ear. "Hi."

Despite what lay ahead of him and their dire circumstances, Cyllus smiled in relief.

Chapter 6

The sedative made her drowsy. Savie regretted taking it, but how could she know a stranger would reveal his own answers to her random journals. Savie knew she'd be taking a risk if she opened the door. But the man, Cyllus, had listened to her journals. Someone had heard her words and come.

Desperation lent urgency to her fingers. The digital lock was easy to disengage. She turned the cool metal handle and the door slid open. A man dressed in all black stood on the other side of the threshold and stared.

"Hi," she said lamely for lack of anything else to say.

She wasn't sure what to expect from the harsh voice cajoling her on the other side of the door. His tone had been even and factual. Now she had the answer to that silent question. Dark brown hair, brown eyes with gold bands and a broad nose with a bump on the end.

There was a face mask of some sort pushed to the top of his head. The band holding it in place separated his short hair in uneven layers. She had the odd urge to smooth it out.

Cruel lips curved up in a cynical smile immediately dispelling the feeling and Savie wanted to slam the door shut in his face as her pulse raced. This man was dangerous. The aura practically bled from his pores. She wasn't even sure she'd be able to close the door in time.

They stood so close she could see the jagged lines forming thick scars in the shape of the letters CR on his left cheek. When he noticed her attention there, his gaze flickered as if afraid of her response.

That small sign, a hint of vulnerability from someone who looked like a hard edged killer reduced her fear dramatically. No one liked to be judged on their appearance, be it good or bad.

Her hand rose of its own accord to touch. The brown eyes gleamed brighter in intensity. What was she thinking?! Savie hesitated with her arm suspended mid-air. He could rip the limb from her and beat her to death with it.

Time froze. Mere inches separated her hand from his face. He held still and didn't move back, a hint air of desperation flaring his nostrils. Did he want her to touch him as much as she wanted to? In the end, her curiosity won out.

Savie's fingers shifted the slightest bit and brushed the cool skin of his bronzed flesh. "You came? You're here?"

He nodded, causing her hand to stroke over the scar. The bumpy edges of the letters grazed her fingertips like a rough brand. Her heart clenched. Who would do such a painful thing to another living being?

"I came. I'm here."

So many questions bombarded Savie, things she wanted to say. Words bubbled to her lips, but she pushed them down. She let her hand fall to her side and peered beyond him toward the hall. No *jobas*.

"Are you here alone?" he asked in a deeper voice.

She could only nod in response. He held his hand out to her. "We need to go."

Cyllus. He'd told her his name was Cyllus. Displaying an unnerving sign of trust, possibly due to the sedative, Savie placed her hand in his and he squeezed. She managed a small grin in response. Then he let her go and shouldered off his pack. When he dropped to a knee in front of her, she asked, "What are you doing?"

They should be leaving before the *jobas* returned.

"Put this on. It will add another layer of protection for your skin." He removed his black jacket and handed it to her.

The bulky leather would drown her frame. Savie slid her arms in the sleeves and pulled the collar up to her nose, inhaling the delicious aroma emanating from the material. She couldn't place it but it was warm, if sensations had a smell. Deep, dark and rich like a fine liquor from back home.

She gave herself over to the sensation and sniffed again, feeling her courage solidify from the scent alone.

Next, he gave her a clear mask with a strap on the back similar to his. "Here. Slide this on but don't pull it over your face until we head outside."

Savie sensed the urgency behind his quick and efficient movements though his voice remained steady when he spoke to her. She set the mask on top of her head, grimacing at the grimy feel of her dirty hair. There was no where to shower in the lab and she'd been making do with wiping off or drinking what there was until the water ran out.

She was sure she smelled like rotten fruit but he didn't react or seem to notice.

Her rescuer stood slowly and eyed her from head to toe. Savie wore Stefan's spare clothes, hers in her room on the other side of the facility.

The plain lab outfit in tan didn't compare remotely to the sleek black pants and dark shirt neatly tucked into the waist that he wore. There were weapons on a holster about his chest and a row of small cylinders hung from the narrow belt on his waist.

He reached forward and zipped up the jacket, offering her a small smirk. "It will do. Stay behind me."

A flutter of fear returned at the thought of running across the *jobas* again. Savie's limited experience with the animals left her petrified of being cornered and eaten or poisoned by their tails.

"What is it?" Cyllus asked.

Savie nibbled her raw, chapped lips, then blurted, "The *jobas*. They have poison on the barbs of their tails. Several of my lab mates died from it."

"I won't let anything hurt you."

He said it as a fervent vow and without knowing him, Savie believed him. That wasn't normally like her. She wasn't naïve. She didn't just go off and follow strange men. Then again, nothing about this entire experience seemed normal anymore. Aliens had come to Earth after an infection that turned people into zombies. That in itself was a lot to take in.

She'd left the world she knew far behind to venture into space. Now she was about to run off with another...alien, she assumed though he looked very human to her.

Yet, he'd listened to her journals and remembered specifics. Enough to share personal things about himself after admitting he didn't like to be vulnerable.

"Alright. I trust you," she told him.

His brown gaze lightened as if she'd said the right thing. He grabbed her hand and tugged. "Good. That's very good. Let's go."

Making sure to stay behind him, Savie followed. Her heart pounded hard enough she expected to see her skin vibrate as they passed the bodies of the *jobas* he'd slain to reach her. Savie slowed. This was her first time taking in a close up look without being frightened at the creatures that had terrorized her team for weeks. A good dozen lay scattered about.

"Hurry," he whispered as they neared the door and moved faster.

She didn't have to direct him, his steps sure as he guided them toward the main exit. Suspicion reared its head. How did he know the layout of their lab? Was he working with the Elusans?

No. He couldn't be. Those beings had appeared in the form of glowing energy figures, their bodies without a physical form. Her thoughts grew cloudy as she worked to resist the effects of the sedative.

Beyond the glass window at the center of the exit door, Savie could see the bright light from the exterior artificial sun the Elusans helped them to install when they'd first arrived. It didn't give off any natural heat as Algor 1 had a balmy even temp year round. Or so they'd been told by their not so helpful benefactors.

Thinking of that time seemed so long ago, but it had only been weeks. Weeks of excitement fading to concern. Concern becoming downright frustration when the aliens who'd led them here failed to respond to their calls. Then the terror. God. Each of them had been so afraid of being trapped and dying on a deserted planet.

Cyllus hit the door release and it opened. Fresh air flowed through on a gentle, soft breeze. Savie closed her eyes and inhaled her first breath of fresh air in weeks. None of the manufactured stuff recycled in the lab ventilation system.

Growling suddenly erupted outside from the left. Savie stiffened and opened her eyes. The sound brought back vivid memories of the attacks.

Twisting around, Cyllus shoved her to the right, causing Savie to stumble. Rapid laser fire followed, then a thump thump. The lunging *joba* hit the ground on its back, four limbs twitching in the air before it died.

Tremors rocked her body and Savie stood frozen. How easily he took down one of the animals who had continuously terrorized her and her team. Nightly howls and high pitch barking had made it near impossible to sleep from the moment they set up the dome facility. They'd been stalked like prey with no line of defense.

Just remembering those times held Savie in a state of shock. Now another one of those foul demons had gotten what it deserved. Her hands balled into tight fists. Slumped on its side, the creature appeared harmless, but Savie knew that was far from the truth. It was a vicious killer.

Cyllus grabbed her by the forearm, urging her into a trot. He kept glancing around them as they ran and spoke in a harsh murmur, "We can't hesitate. Those with me are waiting. We've got twenty minutes to reach where the ship is waiting or they'll have to take off. Another unknown ship is approaching and it's armed with more firepower than the vessel we're on."

An unknown ship? What were the odds of two ships coming when Savie had begged, prayed for rescue? Her side started hurting and she pressed one hand to it while Cyllus kept her other one in a tight grip.

"Don't let their tails touch you. Their sting is venomous," Savie reminded.

"Understood."

She ran as fast as she could and knew it wasn't fast enough. Her weakened condition didn't help. Pebbles and gravel stung through the thin soles of her shoes, creating additional darts of pain. It was no use. Her pace slowed and her feet tripped over themselves. She was exhausted and at the end of her rope. In between pants, Savie managed to say to the looming man at her side, "Leave me."

There was no reason he should die with her. No reason he should be poisoned or torn apart. Savie had seen those deaths. It wasn't a good way to die by any stretch of the imagination.

"Never." Without breaking stride, Cyllus whipped an arm about her waist and hoisted her into his arms.

"Whoa!" Savie linked her arms around his neck and held on, face buried in his throat to block the wind and grit flying in her eyes. She should pull the mask down over her face but didn't want to let him go.

"Not long," Cyllus said. "Ten more minutes and we're gone from here, Savie."

She believed him. Savie held tighter and took deep breaths, using his scent to keep her from a total freak out.

"Shit!" Cyllus let loose more profanity and Savie risked lifting her head to see what happened.

Long howls rang out. Behind them *jobas* gave chase in leaps and bounds toward them. Dust kicked up in swirls about the animals' feet as they sped across the dirt terrain.

On the left, two more rushed in their direction, heads lowered, teeth bared in menace. Savie cried out when she spotted more on the right. At this rate, the creatures would surround them. It was how they worked. Surround and conquer.

"You're alright. I have you, Savie. Nothing will hurt you." Cyllus tightened his hold about her, his hands rearranging her legs to grip him around his hips.

Sucking in a breath, Savie adjusted with him. Now was not the time to notice the prominent bulge at the apex of his thighs. She knew about adrenaline fueled arousal. It worked both ways and she clamped her teeth down on a moan threatening to escape.

The change in position freed up his hands and Savie could do nothing but hold on. Cyllus gripped a laser in each hand, firing non-stop. Looking over his shoulder, Savie flinched. One of the *jobas* behind them gained speed and surged ahead of the pack, haunches bunching with ground eating strides.

Suddenly, it leaped into the air. Visions of claws raking his unprotected back made Savie scream, "Cyllus!"

Spinning about at her cry, he shot the *joba* dead center. It dropped. One hand cupped Savie under her hip. "Hold on."

Her ears rang with the zapping sounds of his lasers. Snarls, howls and growls rose in volume.

"Almost," Cyllus muttered. He unclipped several items from his waist and tossed them behind him. Small balls tumbled to the ground and exploded on impact.

Yelps and cries as more *jobas* fell in the small, fiery blazes the tiny bombs created.

The whirl of engines joined the noises filling Savie's existence. Ahead of them, a ship with a ramp extended awaited. There were three men and a woman dressed in dark clothing lined in front of the ramp. From this distance, Savie couldn't discern any of their features clearly.

If someone had asked, Savie would have sworn they couldn't go any faster. Cyllus proved her wrong. He gained speed, bringing them within yards of the group. Everything passed in a blur and wind whipped at her face.

Excitement tickled her empty belly. So close to being off of this awful, awful planet. Tears streamed down Savie's face. Her fingers curled into the material of Cyllus' shirt.

Another foul curse slipped from his mouth. He lowered his face next to hers. "Can't reload the power cells for my lasers. I won't let them get you."

Savie didn't get the chance to figure out what he meant before they went down in a tumble. Cyllus rolled and his body curled around her. The world spun in a dizzying array.

"Cyllus, what—"

His body jerked above her as his mouth contorted in a grimace. Their eyes caught and held. Regret. Why was his gaze filled with regret?

Cyllus shoved her face into his chest, blocking her view, but Savie heard.

Growls. Thumps. His body rocked over her but Cyllus' arms stayed around her like steel bands, covering Savie with his larger frame. Protecting her.

Shouts came closer. Weapons blasted all around her and Savie muffled her cries. She had no idea what was going on but Cyllus was hurt. She knew it. Knew it down to her bones.

Don't die on me, please, she begged silently.

***

The animals pursuing them must have a fierce pack mentality. Instead of giving up, they chased him and Savie with predatory focus. Cyllus opened his NNP and reached out to Kelix. *"Little help."*

"You blocked me." Kelix's tone was shocked and livid. Mostly livid.

"Not now, Kel. I have the woman but at least two dozen of these creatures are on my heels. They aren't giving up until they get the meal they thought they had cornered."

That's what Savanna Monroe represented to those animals. There was no other explanation for the actions of the native creatures she referred to as *jobas* intent on going after him and Savie.

"We can't leave the ship unguarded. Get as close as you can and we'll cover you."

"How far is the other ship?" Cyllus asked, adjusting his grip on Savie in his arms. Her quiet cries dug like razor sharp blades into his heart.

"It will reach AB476 in less than an hour. Sora attempted to hail them but got no response."

Which made the approaching vessel an enemy. They couldn't afford to be caught and hauled back to Kirs.

Cyllus poured on more speed, shooting at everything moving for them. One of his lasers powered down with a whine. The power cell died and he didn't have a free hand to reload. He refused to put Savie down. They'd tear her apart and he promised to protect her. Cyllus wouldn't break his word.

The ship came into view. Kelix, Reo, Sora and Tagan stood outside waiting. As soon as the *jobas* were in range, his fellow cyborgs began picking them off.

Cyllus lowered his face next to hers. "Can't reload the power cells. I won't let them get you."

Cyllus stripped several shock grenades from his waist belt and threw them behind them. They took out six by his estimate. The concussive booms barely slowed the rest of the pack down. How many of the damn creatures were there?

"You're getting slow in your old age. Behind you," Kelix remarked as he aimed and fired.

Savie screamed almost blowing his auditory circuits. Cyllus spun with her in his arms and shot the animal launching at them.

He turned back around and raced to the ship at his maximum speed. He'd sustained damage but nothing that wouldn't self-repair within the next few hours. If they got out of this.

No, when not if. Cyllus had to believe they would make it. He hadn't managed to save his mother and sister or his pod members, Kaito and Xion, but he wouldn't fail Savie.

"Cyllus!" Kelix roared his name aloud and across his neural net.

Three *jobas* hurdled toward him. His second laser powered down as well. They were too far away from the ship to make it. Kelix and the others ran to intercept, shooting eerily in sync as their cyborg training kicked in. Pod group or not, they'd been designed to work in a team structure.

Jobas dropped around him. More and more of the snarling animals seemed to come from everywhere. If enough of them gathered, the creatures would have them surrounded. Savie would be vulnerable but Cyllus would recover if they severely injured him.

Choice was limited if they were to survive. There was only one option. It would hurt but Savie would make it out unscathed. Cyllus dropped to the ground and covered as much of Savie's body as he could. This was going to be bad.

The first *joba* hit him square in the back. The other two went for his legs and arms, razor sharp teeth digging deep to tear into his flesh through his clothes. Cyllus suppressed his pain sensors and stared at Savie. Her face was pale, lips split and dry.

Scanning showed she suffered from dehydration and other physical deterioration caused by lack of food but her eyes blazed with life. A life Cyllus sought to save.

"Cyllus, what—"

Another bite at the center of his spine made Cyllus want to arch away, but he couldn't. He shoved Savie's face into his chest and curled tighter around her.

Blood loss, laceration, lower left fracture. He cataloged the injuries as they occurred. All repairable. Kelix would see to it.

A lucky claw or tooth punctured him in the side. Blood gushed. Bad. This was bad. His processors fired at maximum capacity. Too much damage for his nanobots to keep up with and repair.

"Safe. You're safe," he whispered to Savie.

Death stared Cyllus in the face. His gaze went to Savie's distressed expression. Her full lips tempted and he remembered the thought he'd had earlier. For Savie, he could find enjoyment in kissing.

Systems faltering, Cyllus gently brushed his mouth along hers in a fleeting touch he wished could be more. A taste, a small taste of her he took and wrapped the memory of it deep inside. Then something slammed into his head and Cyllus' world went dark as his system went offline.

Chapter 7

While Savie tried not to be a crier, sometimes the moment just plain called for it. Like now. They were going to die. So she embraced her fear and sobbed as the *jobas* surrounded them. In her heart, she realized what Cyllus had done by going to the ground and wrapping her in his arms.

Every worry, every wish she'd ever had gloomed like a black cloud, overwhelming her in a tidal wave of emotions.

A stranger, a man she didn't know was willing to sacrifice himself in an attempt to save her. How many more would die to see that she lived? Savie clutched his shirt tighter and pressed her nose directly against the fabric. His sweat combined with his masculine musk filled her nostrils.

Despite what was happening—the attack, the situation—his heart beat like a steady drum. The cadence, however, didn't level out Savie's increased breathing. If anything, it made it worse. Was he giving up? How long before the *jobas* reached her?

Savie sniffed and scrubbed her tear stained face against his damp shirt. Growls bombarded from all sides, the hoarse barks loud and toe curling. Cyllus jerked and twitched but there was nothing she could do to help him. More tears fell until her chest heaved with each exhale.

Cyllus leaned his face against the top of her head. The palm of one hand cupped the back of her head. "Safe. You're safe."

Savie wanted to believe him. She really did. His lips glanced against hers in an unexpected kiss, his mouth cold compared to the heat of his body on top of hers. Savie's lips parted on a gasp.

Suddenly, he gave a deep groan, the sound sending terror lashing through her body. His weight slumped atop her, shoving the breath from her lungs.

Panicked, Savie clawed at his shirt and screamed. It was as if a two ton truck had landed on the center of her chest. Spots flickered across her vision and she screamed again with what little breath she had left. Relief came moments later. Savie inhaled sharply, gulping for air gratefully.

Cyllus was gone. Savie blinked at the hazy blue sky above, the ensuing silence as loud as the howling and shooting had been. Footsteps replaced the growls. Barked orders Savie couldn't make sense of came from someone as they drew near. She curled to her side and slowly sat up.

Three men and a lone woman crouched on their knees in a circle around Cyllus. He lay unmoving on the ground next to her while one of the men began yanking him up by one of his arms. Their expressions remained stoic but the one with a dark glower cursed in a seamless stream as he heaved Cyllus' unconscious form up.

"Cyllus!" Savie scrambled to crawl toward him but the giant with the pitch black hair and midnight eyes paid her no mind and slung Cyllus' limp body across his broad shoulders in a firemen's carry.

"Let's go!" he snapped. "We need to take off. Now!"

The others followed his command. Savie sat back on her haunches in shock. Numbness set in. One of the men leaned down and gripped her forearm. She was rudely yanked to her feet and dragged along.

"Hey! Hey!"

No one listened. Green eyes glared down at her from his immense height. "Cyllus insisted on saving you. That means you're coming with us."

His snarled words grated against her skin, the menace underlying his statement enough to make Savie clamp her mouth closed on any other protest she had. Besides, she had no problem leaving here. At all.

Savie half-trotted, half-ran to keep up. They took the ramp in leaps into the belly of the ship. The door whirled closed. She glanced over her shoulder but couldn't see anything. It was a solid block of dull gray.

The man holding her with a death grip pushed and shoved Savie down a hall and into an open section. The woman sat in a seat, hands a blur as she flicked switches and swiped fingers over a holographic screen displayed directly in front of her face. The dark-haired man practically tossed Cyllus into another chair. Belts came from the slits of the seat to harness him in place. His tawny hair fell forward, blocking a clear view of his face from Savie.

Pitter-patter drops of blood hit the floor beneath Cyllus' chair. Fear slammed into her once more. Even in this dull in between state of shock, Savie knew he was hurt grievously.

"Here." Another snarled direction.

Savie received a hardy push and dropped into a seat that unfolded from the wall. The two remaining men sat. They worked with grunts, commands and rapid speech Savie found it hard to follow. Not due to her translator, which the Elusans had implanted in her team right away. More like they understood one another with minimum speech necessary.

Savie gripped the arms of her seat as the ship came to life with a rumble. Daring to speak, she asked, "What's going on? Shouldn't we get medical care for Cyllus?"

Once more, no one answered. Her brows drew down into what she hoped was a fierce scowl. "Hey! He saved me. Can we at least get him some help?"

The one who'd carried Cyllus darted a look over his shoulder to glare at her. Savie shivered from the heated gaze but tipped her chin up, refusing to be cowed. His upper lip curled at her posturing. "This is your fault. You and your *journal*."

He sneered the last word and Savie flinched back. Such rage. She'd never crossed someone exhibiting this much anger toward her. Then his words hit. Her journals.

Shaking inside, Savie pushed back. "Cyllus needs help. Please."

"I know what Cy needs. Now sit back and shut the fuck up while I concentrate."

Savie's lips parted. To argue or complain, she wasn't sure.

The woman interrupted, "The other ship is in range. Still no answer to the hails. Unmarked identification codes. This isn't Kirsians on our tail."

"Mercenaries then," the dark-haired one supplied. "Tagan, how much firepower do we have?"

The answer came from the man who had snatched Savie up and forced her to follow. "Not enough for an all out fire fight, but we do have some weapons capabilities. Use the hyperdrive."

"That will take up a large portion of our fuel source."

"Do we really have a choice, Kelix?"

Kelix. Savie assumed that was his name. He pressed his lips together before answering. "Fine. Sora, plot the course."

The woman nodded. "Five minute countdown."

"How close are they, Tagan?"

"Ten minutes out," Tagan said. "It's going to be close. They'll catch sight of our tail but once the drive kicks in, we'll be gone before they can do anything about it."

"Three minutes," Sora announced.

Based on their conversation, Savie figured there was still a strong chance she'd die. Instead of being eaten by wild animals, it seemed her new choice was death by fiery space explosion. She grimaced. Neither was acceptable.

Savie turned in her seat and stretched her arm across the aisle until she reached Cyllus' limp hand. No one seemed overly concerned about him.

At least blood no longer dripped onto the floor. That had to be a good sign. Maybe. She entwined their fingers and held on.

"One minute," Sora counted off.

"Missile launch detected," Tagan stated.

Savie's head snapped up. Still no extreme reaction from the group. Muffling a whimper, she squeezed Cyllus' hand and wished he'd wake the hell up. He was the one she trusted. Just the sound of his voice would go a long way to reassuring her.

"Impact in three," Tagan said.

"Hyperdrive engaged." Sora smacked her palm down and the ship surged forward.

Pressure slammed Savie back against her seat. Her face stretched, the skin pulled tight. Closing her eyes, she uttered a prayer under her breath.

***

"Cyllus, need your help here."

Kelix words come across the NNP loud and clear. Cyllus sensed his systems rebooting at the same time. Pain. His nerve endings lit with a barrage of pain.

"Welcome back, buddy," Kelix said.

"Fuck," Cyllus groaned. *"What's wrong with me?"*

"A lot." Kelix clucked like a worried mother. *"You need a power boost to heal faster than your nanobots can repair you."*

Cyllus grunted and tried to turn on his side.

"Hey, I think he's awake."

Feminine voice. Soft but excited. Cyllus opened his eyes to narrow slits. A dirt streaked hand smaller than his own held tight to his fingers. His muscles clenched involuntarily.

"Ow."

He followed the sound to a face. Her grimy features winced. Cyllus released his hold instantly and sat up with a lurch. This female was important. He hadn't meant to hurt her.

"Whoa!" Kelix planted a hand on his chest and shoved him down flat on his back again.

Cyllus stared at the woman. Her information downloaded with a click and all of his memories of her returned in an instant. "Savannah Monroe from Earth. Savie."

She grinned. "Yes. That's me. And you're Cyllus."

Someone had given her a hair tie. The black mass was pulled back in a long tail down her back. Probably Sora. The rest of them didn't have long hair and a need for such.

Savie sat in a chair to the side of the bed he rested on. Cyllus exchanged a look with Kelix and switched to NNP communication. *"What happened after I shut down?"*

"Tagan brought the female with us since you spent so much effort to retrieve her. You took a lot of damage from those animals. You need to connect to the power source and rejuvenate your energy reserves."

"Thank you," Cyllus told his friend as he swung his legs to the side of the bed. He extended his arm and flexed. A small port opened on the underside of his wrist. Kelix pressed a long cable to the port.

As cyborgs they could absorb energy in various ways. Kelix was the one who'd discovered that opening a connection and a direct line via port worked quickest with the least amount of problems instead of absorbing it through their skin with a grip to the power source or other external means.

Once completed, Kelix stepped back. "Done."

This wasn't new to him. Cyllus clenched his fingers and initiated the power feed. His systems flared as the first of the electrical flow hit him. He inhaled and let the rush of pure energy settle over him, then turned his gaze to the woman.

"Savie." He couldn't help how he breathed her name.

"Cyllus." She eyed the cable connected to his wrist. "You were hurt really bad saving me but your friends said you'd be fine."

Touched by her concern, Cyllus used his free hand to stroke her chin and tipped her face back toward him. There was no such thing as the cold when he was near her. "Kelix and the others know how to care for me."

She nodded. He waited for her to say something about the power feed but she didn't. Wanting to avoid an awkward exchange, he asked, "You said there were no others with you?"

"No. I was the last."

The last. Her earlier journal entries mentioned a team. He wanted to question her further but she finally worked up the courage to motion toward the cable sending currents through his arm. "Is that part of taking care of you?"

"Yes. It comes with being a cyborg."

Her throat moved up and down as she met his gaze and swallowed. "Yeah, you mentioned that. Not quite sure how to take it. We don't have those where I come from. I mean, the technology for cybernetics has grown with artificial limbs but not enough to categorize someone as an actual cyborg."

Savie's pulse rate elevated, her respiratory functions higher than when he first came face to face with her. All signs of nerves. She babbled when unsettled. His heart lightened at the discovery. Everything he learned about her was a balm to his battered spirit.

"We are Kirsian. The Military Elite on our homeworld has long been filled with enhanced soldiers."

Her eyes drifted to the cable and the port inserted on his wrist. "Is that...is that going to fix you?"

Cyllus took in his physical condition and ran a scan. Aside from his destroyed clothes, his body had already started the healing process. Analysis complete. He was seventy-five percent healed. In another fifteen minutes, he'd be back to one hundred percent.

"Our ability to recover from injuries has been increased exponentially due to nanobots. We can repair most damage to our bodies but at times, if it is severe, feeding directly from energy speeds the process. We don't take all of our nourishment from food."

Beyond Savie's shoulders, Kelix rolled his eyes. *"Tell her all our secrets, why don't you?"*

"She is different. From a strange world we've not heard of, abandoned by Elusans who haven't concerned themselves with others in decades. There's more to the story of them leaving a group of her people on AB476."

Kelix tensed and he shifted to stand directly behind Savie. Perfect position if he chose to snap her neck. *"Then we should end her before she can enact whatever plot she's been sent to instigate."*

End Savie? Anger filled his core. No one would end Savie. In a flash, Cyllus ripped the cable from his arm and stood. "Do not!"

Savie flinched and dropped his hand. She pushed up from her chair and half turned. "What's going on, Cyllus?"

Cyllus wrapped an arm about her waist and pulled her snugly against his side. She didn't resist. Keeping his gaze on his friend, he answered aloud, "Now that Kelix is assured of my well being, he is leaving."

Via their neural net, he added, *"Do not seek to threaten her, Kel. My response will be to defend her."*

Kelix gaped. *"Against your own pod? We are brethren."*

"And she is something important to me as well."

"You just met her! You don't know if she's a trap meant to lure all of us to our death."

"Savie isn't working with Emperor Shui. She's innocent of everything aside from trusting the Elusans."

"If she's innocent, why is the language from her world uploaded in our translators? That's not Standard we're using with her. It's some convoluted speech. The words don't often match their

meaning. Someone else had contact with her people, Cy. Think about that."

Kelix inclined his head to Savie and spoke. "My apologies if I startled you. I'm going back to the bridge and see where the nearest travel station is. Maybe we can drop you somewhere."

Savie stilled in Cyllus' arm. Kelix spun on his heels and left them alone in Cyllus' room.

Chapter 8

When Kelix left, the chill his presence gave off dissipated. It wasn't hard to read the glint in his black eyes. He didn't like her. Savie had no idea why. Then again, none of the group with Cyllus seemed to care for her. On the bridge, all of them had eyed her as if they'd love to take her back to Algor 1.

A shiver rocked her frame. She never wanted to go back there.

"I'm sorry if Kelix upset you."

Cyllus' rumbled apology vibrated along Savie's back where he'd pressed himself against her. The arm about her waist was a warm weight she wanted to savor. Instead, Savie eased away and he released her without resistance. When she turned around, the heat of his stare had her flushing.

Short for words, Savie blurted, "Thank you."

He arched a brow and waited.

"For saving me. Thank you for answering the emergency beacon. I'd given up hope of anyone coming for me."

His gaze softened. "You are very welcome."

Savie jammed her restless hands under her armpits and avoided his penetrating stare. "What now?"

Would he help her get back to Earth? Savie didn't have many options left. She'd return and have to face the disappointment and humiliating backfire of her career. She could only hope the government didn't press charges due to her leaving with an unapproved separate alien group.

More importantly, with her entire team dead and the Elusans no where to be found, it was her responsibility to inform those families that their loved ones were gone too. Eleven good people filled with excitement and looking to do something wonderful were now dead.

"Would you like to shower? Change clothes and eat?" Cyllus asked, moving away from the bed as he rolled his sleeves down.

Shoving her grief back to deal with at another time, Savie focused on his questions. Food. Clothes. She dropped her arms to her side and rose up on her toes. "Yes!"

One thousand times, yes.

Cyllus cupped her elbow. "Come. There isn't much in the way of food stores but I'm sure we have enough to satisfy your appetite. We'll need to land at a travel station soon and restock."

He led her to a tiny space that was standing room only with one small table bolted to the floor and two chairs. She recognized the cold storage unit with a thin blue light glowing on the door. Cyllus pulled out two containers from inside and cracked the rectangular white packages in half. A delicious aroma immediately filled the room.

Savie groaned, drawing a smirk from Cyllus. She covered her face with her hand and muttered, "Please ignore me."

"Here." She lowered her hand and accepted one of the containers he extended. "It's a carbohydrate noodle meal with sauce reinforced with protein and vitamins."

Her excitement dimmed in light of the dry explanation but Savie followed his demonstration on how to open the sealed fold at one end. There was a spoon slotted inside. She took it out and tasted a scoop. Rich spices and flavors burst on her tongue, followed by a creamy coating she couldn't place.

Humming under her breath, she ate in rapid gulps then blushed under his watchful gaze.

"After you've had your fill, I'll show you where to shower and find something for you to wear. We have a medic unit which can gauge your health status as well."

"Why are you doing this?" Savie finally asked, lowering the empty container and disposing of it in a chute built in the wall.

"I don't know." The gruff mutter touched a spot in Savie's heart. For such a strong figure, he appeared unsure. He tossed the second container onto the table roughly.

Remembering Cyllus' words to her, she knew it was the display of vulnerability he didn't like. Savie cleared her throat. "Okay. Well, we'll circle back to that for later. I'd like to be clean now. In fact, I'm certain anyone who has been near me would like that too."

Injecting humor was the right approach. Cyllus met her gaze and a brief chuckle slid free. "With our enhanced senses, it is common to filter and block out unpleasantness."

Sooo, he agreed she stank? Savie refused to ask. Some things she didn't need to know. As she followed where he led, her mind tried to grapple with what she'd just learned. Cyborgs were real and Cyllus was from another planet. He looked nothing like the militant Vassi with their high fore ridges, solid black sclera and three fingered hands.

Cyllus could easily pass for human, a very attractive one at that. They traveled through several corridors that twisted and turned around corners until he stopped in front of a set of double doors. How big was this ship? The saucer shaped oval hadn't seemed overly large as they rushed inside away from the *jobas* but then neither had the one she traveled to Algor 1 on, yet there had three separate floors on it.

"This is a cleansing unit with multiple use spaces. Very efficient for a vessel of this scale and size," Cyllus explained as he palmed a sensor, causing the doors to slide open.

Savie peered inside and noted the chest high wall closures around four narrowed cubicles. Cyllus entered one and pointed at a silver square plate. "Waste containment."

A sensor must have been embedded here too because a seat rose from the floor. Savie turned quickly away. No need to guess what that was used for. Another wave and the seat lowered back into the recessed section on the floor.

"Here are the cleanser settings." He gestured at a red button and water flowed from the ceiling nozzle in a straight stream.

Huh. No rain head showers. Then again, it was better than the steam and mist cleansers on the Elusan's ship. "Thank you."

He nodded and moved to the cubicle on the right and began undressing. His shirt was ripped over his head with little care and tossed behind him. Savie caught the gleam of muscles and the flex of his taut abdomen when he moved about. Red streaks married his back from the *jobas* bites and claws but nothing like the bleeding wounds from a short while ago.

Next, Cyllus leaned over and slid his pants down his legs. Savie gasped. He didn't wear underwear. Gaze riveted, she watched as he twisted about and stepped out of his boots and pants, giving them the same lack of care as the torn shirt he'd flung to the side.

She must have made a sound or maybe she'd moaned. A little. Cyllus looked up and over the wall that didn't lend itself much to privacy. "Are you not going to shower?"

Startled, Savie spun around, giving him her back. "This is a communal bath, I take it?"

Water turned on and hit the tiles in a steady beat. He was actually showering. Right now.

"My clothes were stained and beyond salvage."

She couldn't help it, Savie peeked over her shoulder. Cyllus' back was to her as he washed his arms and chest with short brisk strokes. Foam built up on his tanned skin in pink translucent bubbles.

The sight of fluffy bubbles on a man as masculine appearing as Cyllus threw her for a loop for a minute but she couldn't tear her gaze away. Foam trailed down his bare chest to disappear below. Water and bubbles competed in a race to run down the arch of his throat, his arms and his torso.

One determined plop of foam hovered on the brown disc of his nipple. Throat dry and palms sweaty in anticipation, Savie waited. She strained so hard she almost tipped over. When the puff of pink finally dripped free, Savie bit her bottom lip and held back a moan.

With a flush, she straightened and jerked her gaze away. Hell and damnation. It wasn't like Savie hadn't showered with others before. Mainly women, granted. If Cyllus didn't care, then it had to be her Earth sensibilities.

She removed the sticky, stained clothes from the lab and cringed at the slack skin and marks on her body. She'd been without food and water for a few days but the impact was there in the small signs.

Hurriedly stepping under the stream of water, it pleased Savie to find the temp moderate. As soon as she rubbed her hands over her body, a soapy film built up. Frowning, she studied the pinkish bubbles on her palms.

"It's a sanitizing cleaner mixed in with the water," Cyllus explained.

She turned toward him again but he wasn't watching her. Did cyborgs have eyes in the back of their heads? She was being ridiculous. It was evident she was the only voyeur in the room. Savie shook away any stray thoughts and got down to the business of getting clean.

***

Thankful his cybernetics enabled him to suppress his erection, Cyllus kept a careful eye on Savie in his peripheral vision. Her stare had heated his body more than the water and aroused him painfully. It took everything in him to pretend to be unmindful of her gaze. He'd nearly broken and launched from the stall to her side when he caught the barely audible moan she muffled.

Savie was in no condition for sex. Not the wild and pounding sex Cyllus tended to favor. While she didn't exhibit outward signs of her fatigue, his sensors continually ran a diagnostic on her and he knew she wasn't at peak health. She needed more food rich in nutrients and proteins. Her drooping lids also implied she was in need of rest.

There were only four sleeping rooms on this ship which meant she'd have to share with someone. The obvious choice would be Sora as she was the only other female onboard. Cyllus vehemently opposed that option. For one, Sora held the same distrust of Savie that Kelix and the others had for her.

Second…Cyllus sighed. He didn't want to be parted from her.

It was as Kelix stated. Foolish and unreasonable but that didn't change Cyllus' mind. The only room Savie shared would be his. He finished showering and turned off the water. They had a limited supply of recycled fluid for cleansing. The tanks would need to be refilled along with other supplies when they stopped.

Cyllus exited the stall and grabbed a pair of folded black pants and shirt from a pile that stayed in the bathing area for that purpose. He spotted similar items in a smaller size. Sora's spare clothing. They each had four sets purchased from their last stop on a pirate's haven last week. She'd gripe at Cyllus, but he'd make sure to pay her back.

He headed to the first stall, where Savie now leaned against the waist high wall support. She'd turned off the water but exhaustion lined her face.

Her head lifted at his approach. "I'm so tired all of a sudden."

Because of the food pouch he'd given her. The meal contained extra vitamins along with a sleep aid. It was for Reo who'd been in decline since discovering none of his pod mates had survived the explosion on the prison transport they'd been on.

The knowledge had occurred not long after their escape. Reo had suddenly jerked upright in his seat on the bridge, groaned and clasped a hand to his chest. When he opened his eyes next, they'd been bleak as he declared, "My pod is gone."

It was a hard blow and Cyllus didn't want to contemplate how much pain he had to be in. Reo barely spoke since then and seemed inclined to give up. None of them would allow that to happen. Circumstance had bonded them. They might not be from the same pod but until they found the others, those still alive, and took down Shui, they had no choice but to survive. None of them would let Reo go easily. He was their responsibility whether he liked it or not.

Cyllus set the pile of clothes on the wall's ledge and tapped the button next to the water flow. Warm air blasted from the ceiling, drying Savie in a burst. She jumped then laughed weakly. "The Elusans didn't have this."

The Elusans. It kept coming back to them. Cyllus waved his fingers above her head and the air dryer turned off. "I have clothes for you to wear later and something for you to sleep in."

Her head wobbled on her shoulders as she agreed. "Sure."

Concern rose at her unsteady gait as she moved. Cyllus leaped forward, his feet getting wet as he caught Savie in his arms. "Savie!"

She nuzzled along the gap of his buttoned shirt, her nose touching his collarbone. "Just wanna sleee—"

Suddenly she paled and crumpled against him. Cyllus lifted her up in his arms. He jostled her but her eyes remained closed. "Savie?!"

No answer. Cyllus dashed from the cleansing room and ran to the med station and the single repair medical bed inside. It wasn't a full medical room because the ship they'd escaped on was mainly for emergency use only. As cyborgs, they were fortunate not to need this space often.

"Get out!" he yelled, seeing the repair bed in use.

From inside, Tagan lifted the clear shielding and leaped out, clearing the space Cyllus needed.

"Move! I need her scanned." Cyllus didn't care how abrupt he sounded.

"You're welcome for the rescue and for helping to save your female too," Tagan said with sarcastic bite but moved away quickly.

Cyllus ignored him and lowered Savie to the bed Tagan had risen from. He tapped out the necessary programming code on the base of the bed, impatient as the clear shield descended from the ceiling and stopped inches above Savie's naked body.

"Request desired," the automated voice intoned.

"Full scan. Health check. Species humanoid. Race unknown."

"Full scan, health check, initiated."

Cyllus crossed his arms over his chest and glared at the blank screen, waiting for the reading to appear. His surface scans had noted nothing more than nutrient deficiencies. What if he'd been wrong? What if he'd missed something important and she'd been wounded internally from the attack?

"What's wrong with her?" Tagan asked in a reasonable tone from the right of him.

Cyllus didn't shift his gaze from Savie's prone body on the bed. "I'm not sure. She was on AB476 without food and water for several days."

"Did she sustain harm from those creatures?"

How the fuck would he know? His system had shut down during the attack to preserve his life essence and he'd awakened in his quarters with Kelix telling him to power up.

"I. Don't. Know! Tagan. Now shut up and let me see what the med station says."

"Hmm." Unmoved by his aggression, Tagan remained standing beside him.

"Don't you have somewhere to go?" Cyllus snapped. "Why were you in here anyway?"

"Laceration slow to heal on my arm. Probably from when I ripped one of those things off of you. You know, when I was out there saving your female."

His female. Cyllus' shoulders eased. Savie was his female. Did he deserve another chance at protecting a woman? Anyone? He still had no idea if his mother and sister had survived. No contact from Kaito or Xion, his missing pod brothers.

What made Cyllus think he could take care of another when so far he'd only proven to be a failure as a leader?

It's why he hadn't protested Kelix taking over once they'd escaped Shui's transport. The pressure was too much. Cyllus didn't care to lead again. Ever.

"Thank you for the assist in saving Savie and me," he forced himself to say.

"Savannah Monroe from Earth," Tagan clarified.

Tagan had been privy to her journals as well. Cyllus didn't think any of the others had listened and studied them to the extent he had though.

"Friends call her Savie," Cyllus corrected, wondering what was taking the medic station so long for a result.

"Are you her friend, Cyllus? Do you even know what you're doing?"

Cyllus broke his stare from Savie to glare at Tagan. "Do you have a problem with it?"

"Just wondering if you know what you're doing."

Tagan's questions prodded at the doubt Kelix had created with his probing earlier as well.

"I know she needed to be saved. I know she begged for someone to rescue her. We joined the military to protect and serve."

Tagan arched a brow and shifted his hips, so he half faced Cyllus and still had Savie on the medical bed in view. Cyllus didn't like Tagan looking at Savie without clothes on but there was little he could do about that now.

"Protect and serve *Kirs*. Which we did," Tagan pointed out.

Pinching the bridge of his nose, Cyllus heaved a sigh. "Not just Kirs. The oath shouldn't be taken lightly. What we did on Bionus was wrong."

For the first time, Tagan's tough façade cracked. His features flushed with shame. "We followed orders."

It was little excuse. Tagan wasn't from Cyllus' pod, so he didn't know what the other soldier had done or how far he'd carried out the emperor's commands. Many had killed on command. Set explosives at civilian homes. There were things Cyllus didn't want to think about, things he'd done and actions he now questioned in the aftermath. Maybe losing his family was to be his punishment.

If that was the case, it was a just and fitting price. The loss of his mother, sister and pod brethren would last a lifetime. His pain would never end if Cyllus discovered they no longer existed in the world.

"Scan complete. Patient origin Earth." The medical system interrupted his reverie with the announcement.

"Where's Earth?" Tagan asked.

Cyllus shrugged. He'd never heard of the planet until Savie.

"Newly inducted world to the Protectorate. All contact limited and under the guidance of Vassi control," the computer continued.

Vassi. *Fuck.* Those bastards took any encroachment on what they considered theirs seriously. They gave new meaning to battle hungry and were known to tip the scales of war if they fought on your side.

"What's a being from a planet such a distance away doing here?"

"I don't know," Cyllus mumbled, too busy trying to piece his thoughts together. "Computer, list injuries."

"Malnourished, dehydrated, fractured rib, minor swelling frontal lobe, tear to—"

Fractured rib? How had he not known that? He's scanned her albeit surface scans only. What if he'd made it worse by throwing her to the ground when the *jobas* jumped on them?

"Repairs complete. Remains of sleep aid sedative flushed from system. Vitamin stimulants administered via nasal spray." The clear shielding rose to lodge back in the ceiling and the medical computer went silent.

Savie still lay there with her eyes closed. Cyllus eliminated the distance between them and studied her prone figure. Her skin appeared more flush, not as emaciated. Her cheeks had filled out some too. The repair unit worked as well as if she'd had her own set of nanobots. He'd have to see about safely purchasing a dose for her.

Tagan joined him on his right side. "There is little information about her people. I'm running continual scans through the ship's sluggish comp and have set an alert to ping if anything new about Earth surfaces."

"And then what?!" Cyllus snapped, disappointed that his time with Savie could be limited.

Tagan gripped his arm and added pressure to ensure he had his intention. Cyllus snarled but Tagan leaned toward him to speak in a sharp whisper. "Then we contact the Vassi and arrange for a way to have them pick her up."

"Kirs is not a part of the Protectorate."

Tagan's green eyes widened. "You can't be serious. Think about it, Cyllus. If the Vassi discover we have a humanoid from a world they've designated as under their protection, we could be inviting a war. Not just against us but all of Kirs. Our friends and families there."

Savie made a soft sound, her head twisting about on the bed. Her brows pulled down in the middle as if their conversation disturbed her. Cyllus slid his arms under her hips and shoulders. He spared a glance for Tagan. "I'm not going to abandon her because you're afraid."

Turning with Savie cradled in his arms, Cyllus strode from the room. He heard Tagan call out, "You don't know her and you're risking all of us! At least ask how someone under the protection of the Vassi ended up with the Elusans."

Cyllus didn't have an answer for that. He *was* risking them. He knew that and still couldn't change his actions. Savie broke through the coldness. Brought back emotions that, in hindsight, shouldn't have been cut off to begin with.

There was not a drop of regret in him for responding to her pleas for mercy and help. If Tagan thought he'd dump Savie at the first station they came to, he was a fool.

She'd touched a part of Cyllus he thought dead. He wanted to know more about her. Figure out every single detail that made up Savannah Monroe.

Chapter 9

Savie woke in the room she'd been in earlier. Cyllus' room. She sat up in the bed with a groan, hand to her forehead. What happened? The last thing she remembered was showering.

"Would you like water?"

Standing across the room with his legs crossed at the ankles and arms folded over his chest was the man himself. Or rather cyborg. He'd claimed he was a cyborg.

"Savie?" Cyllus cast her a worried look and straightened from his relaxed pose. He strode toward the table next to the bed where she sat and held up a glass with clear liquid.

Water. Yes, she wanted water. Her throat was dry. Cupping the container he passed over with both hands, she gulped the cool drink down, not stopping until it was empty.

"More?" Cyllus asked.

Savie shook her head. It didn't hurt. She patted her sides and chest area. Nothing hurt anymore. Not even the minor aches from their desperate run on Algor 1. "What happened?"

He pulled a chair from the desk against the wall and sat with his legs splayed and elbows on his knees. The pose leaned him forward, close to invading her personal space. "You fainted."

"Damn," Savie muttered, stroking back her hair. The strands slid through her hand like silk. Clean, soft. She fingered the ends. That's right. She'd washed her hair in the shower stall.

Her gaze dropped to the oversized man's shirt she wore. She ran her hands over the hem of the black garment. His? Savie looked up. "I don't know how that happened."

"Exhaustion. You've been through a lot and there was a chemical sedative in your system. It didn't mix well with the sleep aid in the food I gave you. I'm sorry for that."

"Yeah." The sedative she'd injected herself with when she thought Cyllus was a hallucination and expected to die.

Her head dropped as she remembered all her friends were dead. If only the team had followed the protocol set up by the United Territories government. They'd just been *so* excited. Savie included.

Aliens were real. Long distance space travel was viable.

And look where she'd ended up. It kinda brought back the old adage that all things shiny weren't golden or something like that.

Savie sighed and looked back to the man who'd come for her. Handsome, scarred face and all. He wore a shirt similar to the one she wore. The black cloth skimmed his broad frame like a lover while his pants clung to obviously powerful thighs. She clamped her legs together when her lower region tingled.

"I don't know if I can ever thank you."

Cyllus came around and sat on her left. Their hips brushed and touched. He didn't move back. "You don't have to thank me."

The sincerity in his gaze held true. Savie swallowed. "Alright. Um...so do you know how I can get back to Earth? Can you take me?"

Savie had absolutely no idea how far she was from home or if space travel was as simple as it seemed. The journey to Algor 1 had taken six weeks. If Cyllus agreed, she could be on Earth in little over a month.

Cyllus reached for her hand and flipped it over. He rubbed his thumb over her palm and her skin tingled from the contact. She watched as he outlined her fingers, caressing and stroking in turn. When their eyes met, his brown gold orbs glowed with a sensual heat. Her breath caught.

The attraction was mutual. Staring at him in the shower didn't feel as awkward with the knowledge.

Although thinking of sex and with someone she didn't know should be the last thing on Savie's mind. Yet here she sat, next to a cyborg, wearing his shirt and no panties if her sticky thighs were any indication.

"It's not that easy," Cyllus finally said.

"Why?" The word almost came out like a cry, but Savie shoved back the sudden bolt of fear. Would he hold her against her will? Force her to stay on this ship?

No. No, Cyllus wouldn't do that. She wasn't sure how she could be so certain but she was.

"I need to tell you more about my situation to explain why it wouldn't be feasible to return you right now."

That wasn't a definite no. Maybe he meant there would be a delay. "I'm sure a few days won't matter."

He huffed a laugh and let her hand go to heave to his feet and pace away. Both hands gripped the back of his neck as he turned toward her again. "Do you remember what I said when we were on AB476?"

"AB476?"

"The dwarf planet you were on."

"Oh. We called it Algor 1. I didn't know it had another name. The Elusans never said."

Cyllus grunted. "That's another problem to solve. But later. When I spoke to you, I mentioned...things I'd done."

A lot of that time had been a confusing blur. Fear she was losing her mind and resolute in her belief that she'd die there, alone. What else had Cyllus said?

"Favorite color black," she remembered.

The corner of Cyllus' lips twitched. "Yes."

Humor changed the harsh angles of his face. She smiled back. He was handsome, but his expression held a darkness she didn't understand. It made her want to help him the way he'd helped her.

"Is that part of it?" she tipped her head toward his face without pointing to make it more obvious.

The cruel letters CR stood out against his skin and Cyllus made no effort to hide the marks. As if in reflex, he touched the raised brand. "A large part of it, yes. Those on all of the transport ships sent from our world like me also bare the same mark. We received it after being found guilty in a one-sided trial that deemed us criminals for our actions."

A criminal. Had she been wrong about him? Savie had so many questions. "Wh-what actions?"

"It's a long story and not all mine to share but I'll say that I did do what I was accused. For good reason." He snorted and his hands clenched at his sides. "Doesn't everyone say that when caught?"

Savie shoved aside the covers, stood and walked toward him. The shirt's length meant it fell to her thighs giving her enough coverage as far as she was concerned. Her braless breasts swung underneath, her nipples perking up with each glide under the material. Wetness dampened her thighs in arousal the closer she neared Cyllus when her thoughts should be on what he'd just revealed.

Nothing was ever black and white, though. Something or someone had made him do whatever he'd done. The way he'd admitted his guilt without artifice let Savie know that Cyllus was honorable at his core.

Guilt stained his face as he watched her approach. "You're right to want to go home, Savie. I'll make sure you get there. Just not yet. Going to Earth would put us in a precarious position because of your world's new status."

"The Protectorate stuff?" Savie asked, coming to a stop right in front of him. She could feel the heat of his body. If she leaned forward the slightest bit, they'd touch. She wanted to touch. Desperately.

Visions of his nude body in the shower came back. The wet glide of water and soap bubbles as it ran over his slick skin. His hair darkened from the tawny brilliant waves to the sleek shade of a mink's coat. Firm muscles coiled and ready to react. Every bit of it was permanently stamped on Savie's mind.

Cyllus' cheeks deepened with a red flush as if he read her thoughts. Never taking his eyes from her face, he breathed out his next words in a husk. "When a new world that hasn't had prior contact with other life forms joins the Protectorate, every care is taken to make sure they are guided through the step by step process.

"This prevents nefarious beings from taking advantage, stealing resources or convincing the new world to make undesirable deals. Usually, an established world is designated to monitor the contact."

That would be the Vassi. The Elusans had definitely bypassed the proper steps. Lexie had been in charge and pulled their team together when the offer came through to her lab. Darius had been designated lead on the project. They'd each jumped onboard, excited with the whole idea and uncaring why one alien species would want to be secretive about ignoring what sounded from Cyllus like standard practice.

"So if you brought me back, the government might hold you to question your part?"

"Kirs, my world, wasn't involved in what happened to you and your team. It would be easy enough to prove with a few questions, but those questions would involve contact with our emperor who rules our planet. If he discovers where we are, he'll send guards to arrest and return us instantly to the prison planet. The Protectorate would have no jurisdiction to prevent that from happening."

Going with her instinct, Savie cupped his jaw. "For how long?"

Confusion filled his gaze. "How long?"

"How long would you be in prison?"

His lips turned down. "My sentence is a death sentence. All of us. Cyborgs and other rebels have been declared wanted criminals. All information regarding our whereabouts is to go straight to the emperor so he can seize control of us again and put us down."

Savie's jaw dropped. Earth didn't have death penalties anymore. There weren't even a lot of jails. There were other reparation systems set up in place for those who committed crimes. Systems that didn't jeopardize an offender's future ability to maintain a livelihood or disconnect criminals from the support of family members while they were rehabilitated.

Savie's chest squeezed tight but she knew she had to get it out. "Was it bad what you did?"

His hand came up to cover hers, he squeezed and pulled away. "Yes."

Her heart stuttered at the simple answer. The pain and remorse on his face was clear to read. He suffered for his actions, his crimes. "Do you want to tell me?"

"No. Not yet."

***

Cyllus gave Savie the truth and waited to see her disillusionment. To see the enchanting glow on her face fade. Instead, she offered him understanding. Grace. "Alright."

That was it. Just alright in her gentle voice. Cyllus exhaled and shook his head in confusion. He didn't deserve her acceptance.

"You need to come to the bridge. We're deciding where to land. Our resources are low." Kelix tapped into his neural net.

Aloud, Cyllus said, "I have to go speak with the others. Will you be alright?"

Savie twisted about and Cyllus tried to see his room from her perspective. Each of them had a designated space. The rooms had been designed with the guards' comfort in mind and their need for rest.

Along one wall, a glass topped desk was pushed flush against it to take up minimal space. The chair was near the bed from where Cyllus had moved it to sit and talk to Savie. His bed was wide and long enough for him to fit during his rest cycles to sleep.

It was often the site of his nightmares as well while Cyllus struggled to deal with not finding Kaito and Xion. At least they were alive. If they'd perished in the explosion, he and Kelix would have felt it on the shared network across their NNP. That didn't mean they weren't injured or in a dire situation in need of help.

Cyllus didn't have the same level of reassurance when it came to his mother and sister. For all he knew, they'd died that fateful day and it was his fault. His fault for blindly following orders.

"I'll be fine. I feel surprisingly good considering," Savie said at last.

The medical unit repair bed had done its job. She still needed to eat but she no longer looked at the end of her tether. "Sleep and rest. I'll return later."

He took a moment to enjoy the vision of her slender legs as she crossed the room to his bed. She leaned over to pull the covers back and his shirt rose the slightest bit in the back, giving him a glimpse of her upper thighs. Any higher and he'd see her nether lips.

Did her people have hair on their groin region? Kirsian women varied with trimmed hair or permanent removal.

Savie slid under the covers and Cyllus forced his gaze away as she moved to lie on her back, her breasts round globes that swayed unencumbered with each move she made.

"I'll be fine, Cyllus."

Chapter 10

On the bridge, Sora acknowledged him by nodding, Tagan ignored him and Reo's dead stare revealed nothing of his thoughts when Cyllus entered. He dropped into the seat behind Kelix. His friend swiveled his chair around to give Cyllus his full attention. Cyllus braced himself, knowing he'd have to defend his decision about Savie but Kelix caught him off guard with what he did say.

"Sora found somewhere close to land but we might have a problem."

Problem later, location first. "Where?"

"Dianides."

Cyllus lunged to his feet. "Another pirate base full of mercenaries?!"

Tagan chuckled but Cyllus ignored him. "What are you thinking, Kel?"

Kelix leaned back in his chair and steepled his fingers beneath his chin. Black eyes filled with resolve, he never looked away from Cyllus. "I'm thinking we're low on fuel cells. I'm thinking we need to stop somewhere and regroup. Have you forgotten Kaito and Xion are out there?"

"You know I haven't," Cyllus gritted out, staying on his feet.

Kelix flipped his hand toward Sora. "Sora's looking for her pod group too. Have you forgotten about them? What about Tagan? Or are you only concerned about the woman we found?"

"How is going to a haven for thieves going to help with any of that?" It made no sense to Cyllus to risk themselves by showing at a location where a large element of the population was willing to sell their own mothers for profit.

The first pirate base where they ditched their Military Elite uniforms and traded for basic clothing was understandable. No one stayed long at the satellite location and it served its purpose as a go between for those on the run.

Cyllus didn't address the issue of Savie. That was sure to start a fight in front of the others.

"We don't have a choice. Everywhere we go someone will be looking for us." Kelix jabbed a finger at his own face. "This brand is like a calling card. We can hide it or cover it but there's not a single legitimate base, planet or colony in this quadrant that won't turn us in to Shui if they saw it. At least on Dianides everyone is hiding from someone."

Damn it. His friend had a point. Cyllus slowly sank back into his chair as Kelix continued. "Besides, we already voted and all of us said yes. I'm just informing you."

Kelix's amusement was obvious. Cyllus couldn't blame him though. He'd push the issue on going to AB476. This was only a fair trade. That didn't stop his next words. "Even Reo?"

It was a low blow. Cruel of Cyllus to utter them. Reo didn't have a pod to find anymore. His team had died a brutal death trying to escape their prison transport. They'd saved two women by shoving both of them into a single person pod.

It was the last contact and communication Reo received over his NNP from them. Tagan and Sora had managed to badger that detail out of Reo. He was particularly tight lipped about saying any more about the final words exchanged with his pod.

"Reo doesn't care either way," Kelix answered.

Cyllus blew out a breath. They needed supplies. There was no way to avoid the stop. Plus, he needed to figure out how Savie ended up stranded then get her back to her world safely and without drawing the attention or ire of the Vassi onto Kirs. He could ask questions and possibly get an idea on Dianides.

"Fine. I'm in."

Sora's chuckle rang out. "Choice was limited unless you wanted to evac through the hatch."

With no suit. Not likely. Cyllus reluctantly grinned. Tagan stretched his arms high above him then pinned Cyllus with a pointed look. "Now that's done. I've been digging to get more information on the female."

"Savie," Cyllus ground out. Was Tagan deliberately avoiding using her name?

"Right. Savannah Monroe. From Earth. Left with other Earth people on AB476 by the Elusans."

Reo stiffened, drawing their attention. When he didn't add anything, Tagan cleared his throat. "We need to ask her about the Elusans, how they contacted her group and managed to get them away without notice because from all the information I'm picking up, her planet has big red warning signs all around it. They've never had contact with other species off world and the first time they did, it came with an infection that almost decimated a large segment of one of their biggest populations."

Cyllus let the information settle. It matched the little he'd gleamed from Savie directly. "Don't forget the Vassi."

"Right." Tagan glared. "For whatever reason, it was decided that the Vassi would be entrusted with any and all communication to this planet. They take that role seriously and have blocked any travel for the first six months going in or out without express permission. From them."

Whoa. Cyllus' processors whirled as he checked and rechecked everything Tagan said. He had access to the same databases and could pull from the same electronic resources. When he tried to probe deeper, he got the same alert and block Tagan must have run into.

He could hack it. But it would draw attention they didn't need. He also didn't like the idea of going onto the mainframe further for information unless absolutely necessary because Shui had access to that system. Cyllus withdrew carefully, being sure to conceal his presence as best he could.

No one fucked around with the Vassi. Not even Shui was bold enough to cross into the other end of their zone or sector. It would start a war he definitely couldn't win.

"How should we handle her?" Kelix asked.

As if Savie was a problem. Cyllus shot his friend a dark look. "We don't handle her."

"We can't keep her. Authorities are already looking for us." Kelix looked to the others for agreement.

"She could be in danger. Until we have an idea on what the Elusans planned, she should stay with us," a new voice stated.

All of them stilled. It was the first time Reo had expressed an opinion about anything since losing the connection with his pod.

Sora clapped her hands together one time for emphasis and spun around to face her nav display. "There you have it. She stays."

She stays. It was what Cyllus wanted but his skin chilled in eerie premonition and foreboding.

"I know you think I'm against you but I'm not. We need to be safe, Cyllus. Too much is riding on finding our brethren and the others. We can't afford a slip-up and something about that woman is covered in danger."

In this Cyllus had to agree with Kelix but he wasn't willing to part ways with Savie. He was too drawn to her.

***

Savie woke to complete darkness. Warmth emanated from behind her, heating her entire body on one side. She gazed around without moving her head. There was a tiny light giving off a thin sliver of white on the textured flooring.

With minimum movement on her part, she eased her shoulder down and glanced at the solid weight lying next to her. Cyllus stared back at her. She jolted upright only to realize the heavy band about her waist was his arm.

"You're finally awake," he announced.

"Um. Yes." Had he slept beside her?

Cyllus rose from the bed fully dressed. That offered some relief. She, on the other hand, still only had on the shirt he'd given her.

"We docked ten minutes ago. Everyone except you and Reo will leave to scout and barter for supplies."

The lack of vibrations explained what must have awakened her from such a deep sleep. Being on the ship in flight was like being rocked to bed like a newborn. Savie felt more rested than she had since any of this began. The Elusans, the *jobas*, the deaths.

Her breath hitched and she immediately slammed a door down on those thoughts. "Are there clothes I can wear? I left behind everything I owned."

All her momentos and digital images of her family. Gone.

Cyllus reached behind him to the desk and handed over a pile of folded black clothing. "These should fit you."

Savie scrambled from the bed and eagerly accepted the items. "Thank you! Thank you!"

A tentative smile curved Cyllus' lips. "Get dressed and I'll take you to Reo on the bridge and introduce you to the others. Officially."

"Ha!" Savie laughed and yanked the slim pants up her thighs. She really hadn't had a chance to meet his friends. Everything happened so quickly during and after her rescue, from the *jobas* to his injury and then her passing out.

She finished dressing and smoothed her hair as best she could before braiding it into a single rope down her back. "Ready."

Cyllus eyed her from head to toe. "Shoes."

He bent over and picked up a pair of boots similar to his but smaller. Savie eagerly switched out her shoes to put them on. The soles on her flats had been shredded from their frantic flight.

Cyllus nodded when she was done. "Now you're ready."

When they reached the bridge, the other cyborgs glanced Savie's way. She recognized them by face but didn't really have names to put to them. One thing stood out. Each of them bore the same strange marking as Cyllus. The CR lettering branded into their cheekbones.

He'd told her everyone got one but what did it mean exactly? Did it have something to do with Cyllus' admission that he was a criminal?

Cyllus gestured for her to come stand next to him. "Savie, this is my pod mate and friend, Kelix."

Cyllus introduced her to the glowering man who towered over her with his black hair and blacker eyes. How was it possible to have a gaze that dark? It was easy to read his dislike of her. Apparently, nothing had changed from their first hurried meeting but he nodded and said, "Savannah. Hope you rested well."

"I did." She cleared her throat to remove the rasp. "Thank you. For saving me and helping."

Kelix's arched brows left little doubt it hadn't been his choice. He didn't say anything else after greeting her. Heat flooded Savie's cheeks, so she turned to the only other woman.

She rose from her seat with innate grace and moved closer. Dark hair and silver eyes, she stood almost shoulder to shoulder with Cyllus, her body lean but packed with muscles.

If Savie was back home and hadn't experienced all she had, she'd be properly intimidated. Instead, she was mildly curious about a female cyborg.

Cyllus ran a calming hand down Savie's back. "This is Sora. She is the one whose clothing fit you."

"Oh." Savie patted at the shirt and pants she wore. Sora didn't seem to hate her with the same intensity as Kelix but her expression wasn't exactly welcoming either. "Thank you for lending me something to wear."

The woman shrugged. "Didn't really have a choice. Cyllus had already taken them."

Stung, Savie bit back a sharp retort about kindness. With no money or resources, Savie was completely dependant on them, or rather Cyllus, which meant she wasn't in a position to push back. Yet. She glared at Sora in warning to imply her circumstances wouldn't always be this bad. A sudden gleam of amusement flickered in the other woman's silver gray gaze.

"Tagan you met."

Dark brown hair, green eyes and gruff nature. Savie remembered him for certain. "Hello, Tagan."

"Yeah," he grunted in reply and shouldered a pack on his back as if itching to leave.

"Are all of you cyborgs?" she asked to confirm her thoughts.

No one answered and they all prepared to leave.

"Yes," Cyllus answered on their behalf after shooting his friends a glare.

Sora picked up a pack similar to the one Tagan wore. "We should head out. The sooner we find what we need, the sooner we can leave without worry of being recognized."

There was one person left to meet. Savie eyed the lone man leaning against the wall watching her. No emotion flickered across his face. No dislike, no impatience. Nothing. Just a blank stare that sent a chill down Savie's spine.

"That's Reo. He's staying back with you."

Savi twisted her fingers together and contemplated if she'd be safer going with Cyllus. This one reminded her of a demon waiting to be unleashed from hell.

Chapter 11

Cyllus hated leaving Savie, but Sora was right. They needed to be quick about obtaining supplies and finding somewhere to stash the ship while they searched for information about the others from their missing pods.

When he turned to follow the others, Savie's downturned expression as she worried her bottom lip tugged at him. Once more against his normal behavior, he stopped, reached out and caught her fingers to bring her in closer to him. He leaned over to meet her gaze evenly. She wasn't quite short, but she wasn't nearly tall enough to look at him eye to eye.

Those luminous blue eyes reached inside and locked onto his heart so tight Cyllus didn't bother trying to break free. He let himself fall into whatever this would turn out to be. "Will you be alright?"

After all she'd been through, he expected her to be distraught, yet she hadn't had a meltdown or fallen apart. For someone who came from a world with no prior contact with other humanoid species, she was surprisingly calm.

"I'm fine."

She was. Almost. But not quite. He'd fix that for her one day. Cyllus shifted his gaze to Reo, who maintained his pose, shoulders leaned back against the wall. His attention was somewhere else as it had been of late.

The others filed out, expecting Cyllus to join them promptly. And he would, but first he needed to assure himself that Savie would be here when he returned in the same state he left her.

"Savie is your priority, Reo."

Nothing. Reo met Cyllus' gaze and stared blankly.

"Take care of her," Cyllus ordered bluntly. "That's all I'm asking."

A slow incline of Reo's head. It would have to be enough. Stroking a hand through Savie's hair and tucking a section behind her ear, Cyllus kissed her temple and left.

Outside, Sora and Tagan shot him a look over their shoulders as Cyllus joined them. Heads on a swivel, they took in the crowded, bustling port. Sora had landed in a designated slot at the far end of the travel port station.

"I thought we didn't want to be seen," Cyllus noted. This wasn't the open field he'd envisioned when they discussed hiding the ship.

"Sora filed a plan under a masked ship ID. As far as anyone is concerned, this is an antique disposal vessel," Kelix said.

"Good idea."

All around, ships of every size and design were guided in and landed. Various species were represented in the rushing flow of bodies. Some in uniforms, some in casual clothes. This particular space station's port opened up directly amid the colony's bazaar district so when they walked out, they were in the middle of a vibrant community.

Dianides was known as a place where everything had a price. Overhead signs in glowing lights advertised anything someone could conceive. The air scented of fried delicacies, rich spices and food not created in a replicator. Stall after stall offered hard to find wares and things more common to be bought.

"This way," Kelix said and strode toward their right.

Cyllus hunched his shoulders and ducked low as he followed. Sora covered the rear and pulled up the collar of her lightweight jacket. They slowed near a machine that dispensed credit chips.

"Just as we planned," Kelix muttered. "Don't do anything more."

Sora eased to the front and after checking to see if anyone watched, she placed her palm at the side of the silver plated device and bowed her head.

Soon the hair on Cyllus' forearms rose in response. Tagan twitched nervously beside him. Cyllus felt the low vibrations she gave off with whatever she did with electrical pulses that none of them could match.

"Done," she announced, lowering her arm. A clink clink sounded and a thick black card popped out of the front slot. Two more came next. Sora snatched them free and held them up for their perusal. "I gave us each ten thousand *crusos*. Should be sufficient for our needs."

Crusos was an accepted form of currency in this part of the Eridani sector. They'd traveled to the far end of the Leonides star system to avoid detection by Shui.

Kelix snagged one. "Fuel, food and weapons."

Cyllus took the other, ignoring Tagan's glare.

One of the things they'd voted on unanimously involved upgrading the ship's weapons and purchasing a stronger shielding program. Both would aid in their protection if they ended up in a firefight they couldn't avoid or evade with speed.

At least the ship had that going for it. The hyperdrive was one of the newer designs as long as they had the distance to initiate it before being attacked.

"I'll retrieve food and supplies for the replicator," Sora said, then spun off and vanished into the growing crowd.

"Tagan can go with me to negotiate the weapons. That leaves you to retrieve fuel cells, Cyllus."

Kelix tapped into their shared NNP. *Are you good with handling that?*

"Not a problem." Being alone to complete his task would enable him time to look into the status of Earth and any other information he could find for Savie. For the right price, everyone talked.

They split up, fading into the streams of rushing people. Unable to use his mainframe without fear of the emperor or one of his spies latching on to his location, Cyllus had to manually search for a merchant that would fit his needs. He passed hawkers waving brightly colored glow sticks to draw attention to their tables.

Cyllus stopped by one merchant with a table full of clothing. He eyed the pastel shirts and pants, testing the material for quality. The owner smiled and bowed, his bald head gleaming and the antenna on top wiggling in welcome. When he straightened, his gaze immediately went to the brand on Cyllus' cheek.

Dropping his hand to the laser he carried, Cyllus waited. Choosing to live, the merchant asked, "Help you?"

He spoke in Standard, his accent giving the language a stilted staccato beat. Cyllus responded in kind. "Women clothing. Few pieces."

"Yes, yes. I have many. Teerel help find." Teerel grabbed a purple length of silk for Cyllus' consideration.

Trying to imagine Savie in the long shroud didn't work. "No."

They went through stack after stack until Cyllus ended with three pairs of pants, two in black and one in blue.

My favorite color is blue.

He also purchased five shirts in a mix of long and short sleeves. He'd had to guess Savie's size but if there was one thing a cyborg was good at, it was measuring with accuracy. These would fit.

Teerel tapped the debit card and returned it to Cyllus once the purchase cleared. Tying the items in a fragrant netted satchel, he bowed and left the merchant.

Next up fuel. This was easier to find as the back end of the bazaar had been set up into sections based on product. Off to a corner beneath a rust colored large tent was where mechs sold their wares. Used and new parts for a plethora of machinery along with fuel resources were visibly displayed.

At a glance, Cyllus knew where he wanted to go. He tapped on the tan canvas cover blocking a humbly made doorway. Moments later, the material was slung aside and the owner waved Cyllus in.

Coarse hair in a rich brownish-gold color covered the female's squat body instead of smooth skin. Her red dress stopped above her ankles, revealing bare feet. The top of her head reached Cyllus' midsection. Unlike Teerel, she didn't acknowledge the CR emblazoned boldly on his face. She ambled toward a stool and stepped up to bring her in line with a storage container. "What do you need?"

Cyllus rattled off the serial number for the fuel cells their ship used.

"Uh huh, yes." She twisted about, opened the storage unit and pulled out two solid black canisters. "Eight hundred *crusos.*"

Higher than the norm and what a vendor could request at a legal station but they weren't at a legal station and Cyllus had no choice but to accept the monetary mark up. These fuel cells could last for several weeks. More if they didn't have to rely too much on the hyperdrive often.

Now that the transaction was completed, he could focus his attention on the mystery of Savie. Enhanced hearing came in handy as Cyllus pretended to stroll casually through the narrow passageways, pausing occasionally to observe wares he had no intention of buying. He was close to giving up when he caught it.

"Vassi controlled space..."

"New to the Protectorate..."

And more importantly. "Saw a woman with the mark. Huge reward from the emperor of Kirs on any information about the escaped cyborgs."

"Kelix, we need to leave now. Someone made Sora and is considering the reward."

"Heading back to the ship now with Tagan. Do you have a line of sight on Sora?"

Cyllus hadn't seen her since they parted. *"I'll circle around now. You get back to Reo."*

To protect Savie. Cyllus trusted Kelix the most to make sure nothing happened to her because Kelix, despite his displeasure with her presence, would never let anything happen to someone Cyllus cared about.

And he did care for Savannah Monroe. His feelings had moved from protective obsession to something more. Deeper feelings he had yet to explore.

*****

Savie sat in one of the vacant seats on the bridge, unwilling to be alone with her rampant thoughts in Cyllus' room. The large man with her hadn't spoken since the others had departed. He also continued to stare at her with unerring focus.

"Intimidation is the tactic of bullies," she said when the silence grew too much for even her to bear.

His gaze didn't falter, nor did he relax his vigilance.

"You could tell me a little about yourself," she continued. "What's it like to be a cyborg? Are you and Cyllus good friends?"

Nothing.

Savie didn't let his silence rattle her. She asked questions and talked until her throat grew parched. It came as a huge surprise when he finally did speak and it wasn't to answer any of the questions she'd asked.

"What is your motive?"

His voice rasped against her nerves. Savie shivered and ran her hands up and down her arms. "Motive?"

He pushed away from the door and stalked toward her with heavy steps. "You conveniently send out a distress signal, enthrall one of my companions and hail from a planet none of us have ever heard of. Do you really expect us to believe you don't have nefarious intentions?"

He stopped inches from where she sat, his booted feet brushing the tips of her shoe covered toes. Dead eyes. He had dead eyes.

"I don't have nefarious intentions." Savie swallowed and thought about standing but didn't want him to view her actions as a challenge.

He hovered over her and stated clearly, "Then why are you here, Savannah Monroe?"

Her story spilled out. The Elusans. Her team of friends. The *jobas* and anything else she could think of. When she was done, moisture gleamed in her eyes. Savie swiped at the tears angrily. "So there you have it. I made a foolish decision, trusted the wrong aliens and now I'm alone and have no idea how to get back home."

While she recited her tale, he'd glowered the entire time. Now he crossed his arms over his chest and asked, "What are your intentions?"

She slammed her palms on the armrest and lunged to her feet. He didn't step back and this time she didn't care. Savie stabbed his hard chest with a pointed finger. "I want to go home! That's my intention. Are you happy?"

"Happiness is no longer an option for me," he muttered in a vague manner she didn't understand. He eased back slightly but still invaded her personal space. "Where does Cyllus fit in this?"

Cyllus? "He saved me. You know that. You all responded to my messages."

"He is exhibiting an unnatural attachment to you that places all of us in danger," Reo countered.

Her attention perked up hearing that. Cyllus was attached to her? She was attached to him. Probably due to him being her rescuer but Savie didn't think so. It was more and she didn't want to let him go. Which was foolish because, of course, he wouldn't want to go with her to Earth. If she ever made it back there.

"I don't want anyone in danger. I...I only want to go home."

"And if that's not an option?"

Not return home? Savie had considered that. Before the death of her friends, she'd wondered if she could live in space far away from all she knew. One of the things she'd dreamed of was falling in love and having a family. It hadn't happened on Earth in all of her twenty-six years, so maybe in the recesses of her mind, she'd thought about meeting someone now that she knew a vast world of other races existed.

Facing Reo and his enigmatic stare, she shrugged. "No one can foresee the future. I guess I'll have to see where the chips fall."

His brows lowered. "Your language is a strange one."

He must not have understood the old saying. Savie was petty enough not to explain. Instead, she focused on a tiny detail. "My language. You speak it really well for someone who's never heard of Earth. Maybe I should be questioning *your* motives."

He smirked. "Only a fool would pit themselves against the might of the Vassi military. As a cyborg, I'm competent in my abilities, but I've no desire to be torn limb from limb."

Huh. "The Vassi are that big of a deal? I know they've been helping my world adjust to the concepts of aliens and space travel."

"They used to be a warfaring race. Decades of battles defending those weaker than them on and off their homeworld. Soon, others learned to avoid them or back down from confrontations," he explained to her surprise.

"They're bullies?"

Reo shook his head and lowered his arms. Head tipped up, he stared at the ceiling. When he returned his gaze to Savie, the rigid lines of his face tightened. "They are honorable. They will not mislead your people. Because they live in another sector, Kirs has never had direct contact with them. Beings in the Eridani sector have no need to explore that side."

He tapped his temple and continued. "Translators are universal. The technology spread and shared. The Vassi uploaded the various languages from your planet so that all would be able to communicate with...humans as you are known. That is a sign they expect more of your people to interact with foreign beings and species beyond your boundaries. If their intent was foul, they would not have done so."

Since Reo was in the mood to talk, Savie pushed for more. She might never get the chance again. "What about the Elusans? What can you tell me about them?"

His upper lip curled. "No one can say much about the Elusans. In the past, they had a reputation for an intelligence that surpassed even the smartest worlds. They gave up materialistic life to travel the stars. Soon they gave up their corporal forms. Evolving to the next level has always been their goal and once achieved, they withdrew from what they considered basic life."

"But that's not possible," Savie declared. She glanced helplessly around the bridge. "They came to us on Earth. They offered us the ability to go to Algor 1."

"Algor 1?"

At his frown, she clarified. "Cyllus said you called it AB476."

Reo moved away from her. "I can't explain why they did what they did. Only that you and your friends are the first to have contact with a race long thought dead for decades."

Stunned, Savie staggered back.

Chapter 12

Cyllus spotted Sora in a dead end street off of the main marketplace. Two rough males wearing dark brown cloaks with the hoods pulled up stood on each side of her. They must have realized who she was and cornered her.

With their backs to him, they hadn't had a chance to notice his arrival yet. Steps light, Cyllus came up behind both of them and pressed the tips of his lasers to the back of each of their heads. The stench wafting from their overly large coats made him want to cringe. "Move away from her. Now!"

He barked the last command and they stilled. No startled movement or rush to comply. Sora's widened eyes met Cyllus' over the shoulder of the one on the right. Oil streaks and dirt covered the CR brand on her cheek.

She'd done something to her hair and the mass was contained in several gnarled buns all over her head. It was a decent enough job and she should have gone unnoticed. Her appearance matched dozens of other miscreants here if one didn't pay attention to the muscular form beneath her black clothing.

How had anyone recognized her as one of the escaped cyborgs? Females were often ignored here unless something about them drew attention their way.

"Cyllus!" Sora snapped in a tone he couldn't decipher.

"Come away from them," Cyllus directed while maintaining his attention on the broad ruffians. Neither of the males had made a single move since he came up behind them. Suspicious behavior like that increased his concern.

"Sora, you know you can stay with us," one of the men said.

They knew her name. Cyllus stored that knowledge for later and backed up a half step, weapons still aimed to blow their heads off if they made one wrong step.

"Don't," Sora cautioned.

Was the warning for Cyllus or them? He couldn't tell. She moved in smooth increments to the left, far enough neither man could touch or make a grab for her.

When Sora rounded them and neared Cyllus, she said, "Don't shoot. Brion and Mikal had news of my pod."

"Turn around. Carefully or you *will* die today," Cyllus commanded.

They turned. Large ocular goggles covered the upper half of their faces. Matching black and gray striped scarves hid the bottom half from view. It was hard to distinguish their actual sizes due to the hooded cloaks but their appearance now that he looked at them directly was enough for Cyllus to recognize them for who they were.

Fucking Reapers. How had Sora gotten tangled up with their kind? Men of their ilk made their own rules and dispensed their own form of justice when they felt betrayed.

Nomadic by nature, it was hard to ever track individual members and the level of secrecy within their brotherhood had never been cracked. Not even if one was captured. They preferred death over revealing any truth about themselves or their dark organization.

"We're leaving," Cyllus muttered in an aside to Sora. "Your presence here has been noted."

She sucked in a breath. "Understood. I have what we came for and Brion has shared everything he knows."

Now to figure out how to get away without lowering his guard. Brion watched Cyllus. The one named Mikal spread his legs in a wider stance and pushed back the sides of his cloak to reveal his bare chest and the row of shock grenades hooked to the double looped belt about his waist.

Cyllus understood the threat clearly. "You planning to use those?"

"Maybe," Mikal growled.

"Go!" Brion said. "We have no quarrel with Sora. We wish her well in her search."

Then the two turned and disappeared into the crowd. Cyllus switched to his ocular implants and still couldn't track their presence. It was as if they faded into the wood work.

Rumbles rose in volume behind him. Shouts of discovery. That didn't sound good. Cyllus met Sora's flashing gray eyes. "Run!"

They took off back toward the ship, their speed blurring them to the average eye. To Kelix through his NNP, Cyllus said, *"I have Sora. On our way."*

***

The change rippled over Reo seamlessly. They'd been talking of random things, his tone gruff but no longer aggressive. Then his loose limbed stance shifted to one of readiness. Savie looked around to see if she could tell what caught his attention.

"Our presence has been discovered. Strap in," Reo snapped, moving around her to take the seat usually reserved for Kelix.

Savie didn't question the change in Reo's manner. She sat in a seat and gritted her teeth as the straps for the safety harness crossed her chest, securing her in place. Heart pounding in fear at whatever had caused such a dramatic change in Reo, Savie began begging the universe to give her five minutes of peace for once. Just five minutes.

The ship came to life with a high-pitched whine and rumble. It hadn't done that before. Pulse ripping terror held her frozen in her chair as Savie stared at the door. "Cyllus? The others?"

Did Reo plan to leave them?

"On their way," he answered, head lowered to the panel in front of him. His hands moved in smooth counterpoint to one another.

"Do you know how to fly?"

He snorted and didn't bother answering. Right. Military cyborgs. Of course he could fly. A wave of lightheadedness washed over Savie and her stomach growled. Talk about embarrassment and poor timing.

Something flew through the air and landed on her lap. She glanced down at the silver pouch similar to the one Cyllus had given her to eat before. She tore into the pack with her teeth and used the folded spoon inside to shovel the food in her mouth.

"Is there any reason why we seem to be in a hurry?" she asked between bites.

"The greedy have decided they want the reward offered for information regarding our location. Some more brave souls have decided they can take us in personally."

Stomach satisfied, Savie crumpled the empty packet in her lap. "How do you know?"

"The computer picked up the warning and alert broadcast over the airwaves on Dianides. I monitored the ship's computer."

"Is that dangerous for you?"

"No. Only if I expand my reach through our mainframe," he answered in more detail than Savie expected.

The door to the bridge swished open to the right of Savie. Kelix and Tagan burst in. "Go! Go!"

"Wait! Where are Cyllus and Sora?" Savie cried out.

She'd trusted these people. Would they leave their friends behind? No! She refused to lose anyone else. Rage built as Savie worked to free herself from her harness. Not on her watch. She wouldn't let that happen. She'd fight all of them if she had to.

A warm hand covered her trembling fingers. Savie looked up into midnight eyes, creased in the corners. Kelix. "Cyllus is on his way. You will not need to take us all on to save him."

Savie realized she'd been speaking aloud. She'd actually threatened to fight cyborgs. The tears burst forth without notice. Savie pressed her palms to her face and sobbed. The door wooshed open and closed again but she was mired in her sorrow and didn't look.

"What's with her?" a feminine voice asked.

It sounded like Sora but Savie couldn't stop the flood now that the gates were open. Her harness was unlatched, and she was lifted. Strong arms enfolded her in a familiar embrace. Savie looked up. Cyllus held her and sat in the seat she'd been in with her on his lap.

"Get us out of here!" Kelix shouted.

Sora took the navigation seat and Reo yanked hard on the guide bar. The ship shot straight up. Savie screamed as pressure forced her back into the heat of Cyllus' body. Tagan gripped the back of their seat to reach a free chair and clapped Cyllus on the back as he passed.

"Feels like all we do is run." Catching sight of Savie's appalled expression, he laughed as he did up his harness.

They were crazy. None of this was remotely funny.

"Hold on, Savie," Cyllus whispered in her ear and buckled them together.

It was a rough ride. The ship banked sharply to the left once it reached the skies. Savie viewed it all from the large screen at the front. No one gave chase but that didn't stop Reo from flying as if the hounds of hell were on their heels.

They maintained the excessive speed for what seemed hours. At one point, Reo rose and switched places with Kelix. Tagan had his legs sprawled out in front of him and stared at her.

"Hyperdrive disengaged," Sora announced finally.

The ship slowed and Cyllus undid the harness binding them together. Savie eased away reluctantly and slid into the chair next to him.

"Are you alright?" he asked.

"That was scary," she shared.

He shook his head. "Not that. Before."

When he'd found her bawling like a fool? Lovely. "I'm fine. Everything kinda hit me at once. Again."

"Do you need the med station?" he asked.

"Med station?"

"It's the repair unit that healed your injuries."

From when she'd fainted among other things. Savie offered a tentative smile. "No thanks."

There was nothing wrong with her time couldn't heal.

"You've been through a lot." He stood and held out his hand to her. "I brought some things for you. Why don't you go and rest, eat. I'll bring them later."

Rest did sound like a good idea. Savie placed her hand in his and squeezed. Cy wrapped an arm about her shoulders and kissed the side of her head.

So what if his friends watched her with distrust as their gazes landed on Savie. Cyllus trusted her and it was all she needed right now. "Alright."

She pulled away and headed for the door of the bridge. The others glared as she made her way out.

With the exception of Reo. He didn't lift his head at all. Whatever she'd drawn from him earlier was gone, he'd fully retreated back into his silent watchman pose.

Chapter 13

As soon as Savie left, Cyllus glared at Sora. "What was that about earlier with the Reapers?"

She didn't pretend to misunderstand. "They got a message to me that they had information while I was sourcing supplies."

Cyllus stroked his jaw in consideration. "You trust them?"

Shrugging, Sora said, "Brion and Mikal are former lovers of mine."

"At the same time?" Tagan asked, sitting up with sudden interest.

"Wouldn't you care to know?" came her sharp retort.

Tagan eyed her speculatively. "Hmm. Increased respiration, direct eye contact and narrowed gaze along with answering a question with a question. Definitely together at the same time."

Cyllus waved off the banter and potential argument. Tagan could drive the most calm to fight. "They're Reapers, Sora. You took a risk."

Reapers came and went where their mood took them. Everyone considered them dangerous since they held no loyalty to anyone or anything outside their brotherhood.

"I have a lead on someone from my pod." There was no remorse in Sora's attitude. Pleasure suffused her features at she made the announcement.

Reo lifted his head and his gaze locked on Sora. Envy gleamed in his gaze briefly before he masked his expression and turned back to stare blankly at the wall.

Kelix merely nodded. "Good. That's good. Where?"

"Solus."

Solus was a day's ship travel. They could manage the trip to the large settlement on the planet Vagars with little impact on the new fuel cells and supplies.

"It's a good base. No military presence. The residents are a mix of hard working people and random travelers looking for a resting place. We shouldn't draw attention there," Kelix agreed.

"No place is safe," Cyllus pointed out.

They were quiet as they reflected on this fact.

"I'll set the course." Sora announced and turned to her screen to do just that.

No place was safe but it made the most sense. Ignoring information about fellow cyborgs wasn't an option.

Tagan cleared his throat. "Are we going to talk about the woman? If it won't offend Cyllus, of course."

Cyllus tensed but didn't leap from his seat to choke Tagan for the derisive tone he used. Now wasn't the time to let emotions rule. Temperaments still ran high from their close escape.

To his surprise, it was Kelix who defended Savie's presence. "Having the Earth woman with us shouldn't be a detriment at this point. We aren't in the sector where the Vassi and her race live. As long as we stay under the radar, no one should notice. While on Solus, we'll try to figure out a way to return her to her people without getting thrown under fire."

Since there wasn't anything Cyllus could say to that, he remained silent. Reo rose from his seat and walked out without a word. They all stared after his departing figure.

"What are we going to do about him?" Cyllus asked.

He felt for the other cyborg. It was easy to see Reo didn't think he deserved to survive when his brethren hadn't. He'd lost his pod, blamed himself for not being on the same transport as them to help.

Showing an unusual display of compassion, it was Tagan who said, "Reo could be any one of us at any given moment. Shui must pay for his crimes."

Indeed. Cyllus stood, unable to shake the need to check on Savie. He grabbed the pack he'd dropped by the door during their hectic escape. "I'll be back for my shift later."

Each of them had learned how to fly the ship after observing Kelix and listening to his instruction. Memorizing the basics came easy to cyborgs. This way they could all fly in an emergency if necessary.

Cyllus waved on his way out and strode quickly down the corridor. Unlike the others, having Kelix with him meant he had a member from his pod close by. It wasn't enough but it kept him grounded when thoughts of Xion's and Kaito's fate sought to pull him down.

There was also Savie. Focusing on the female he'd saved blocked the dark thoughts about his mother and sister seeking to intrude.

Cyllus found her as expected in his room. She lay stretched out on his bed on her back, gaze on the ceiling. Her head tilted to the side at his entrance, hair spilled over his pillow in thick coils.

The brush he only used to swipe over his hair in the morning was out on his desk. A few black strands were caught in the bristle and it pleased him to know she used his things for her comfort. Which reminded him. He held up the package he carried. "I brought you something."

Sora's clothes fit her well enough but the pant legs were overlong and Savie had rolled thick cuffs at the ankle. Savie sat up, brows creased in query. "What is it?"

He crossed the space and handed the netted satchel to her. "A few things I thought you might need to tide you over."

She slid the top open with agonizing slowness to Cyllus. He waited breathlessly for her reaction.

"Clothes!" she gasped, meeting his gaze with an excited glimmer in her blue eyes. "You brought me clothes."

"It's only three outfits or so. This way, you don't have to continue to wear Sora's things."

Savie held up the pale blue shirt that matched a morning sky and the navy blue pants cinched at the waist and ankles. She looked up at Cyllus and the heat of embarrassment burned his cheeks.

"Your favorite color," he explained needlessly.

"Cy-llus." The soft way she called his name had the same effect on him as when he'd read her journals.

It made him want to protect, defend. More than that, it made Cyllus want to...love. Since his conversion that emotion had been in low reserve.

Then there was his current circumstances. How could he possibly be thinking of having another life dependant on him?

He was a fool for even having the thought but it was pointless to resist her allure. Savie couldn't understand what he'd do for her.

The strong visceral emotions for a woman he didn't know weren't like him. Yet here he was wrapped in his feelings for Savie. Cyllus cleared his throat and tucked his hands in the pockets of his pants. "Friends call me Cy."

Savie leaped to her feet and wrapped her arms around him. In no way could Cyllus have anticipated her reaction. He pulled his hands free and jerked her close. Sensations so intense he couldn't track all of them rolled over him, settling in his core. He closed his eyes to better appreciate them. Warmth. Acceptance.

Her touch encompassed all of those feelings and sent them directly into his bloodstream like bolts of energy during a feeding from a power source. Her body curved into the arch of his.

They fit like two halves finally put back together. More. Cyllus wanted more of this unconscious healing.

Savie tipped her face up and her parted lips tempted him with savage fury. Restraint broke. On a muttered growl, Cyllus lowered his head and kissed her. He stroked his tongue into the recesses of her mouth, tasted the tang of a reheated meal pack mixed with the sharp, crisp bite that was all Savie.

He memorized her scent, her taste, storing each tiny detail in his memory banks so he'd know her anywhere and could replay them later. Savie moaned and slid a leg along his calf, continuing until the strong limb rested around his thigh. Cyllus hefted her higher in his arms, the position pressing their groins together.

With his erection nestled in the cradle of her center, he paused and shuddered. Cyllus didn't want to move. Groaning, he pulled back from the heated kiss and placed his forehead against hers. His processors whirled with his elevated body stats. He was far from the rigid, cold cyborg of weeks ago.

Breath coming in jerky gasps, Savie slid her fingers through his hair and brought his head back down. "Please."

He couldn't refuse her. Desire ignited like a raging blaze and Cyllus gave in on a snarl, savaging her mouth.

Their second kiss was as potent as the first. Cyllus locked his hands about her hips and stumbled his way toward his bed. He directed their fall, spinning them so he landed first with Savie lying atop him.

They attacked one another's clothing. Tugging, pulling until hands met bare skin. Cyllus smoothed his hand up Savie's torso and fondled a full breast. Her nipple hardened in the center of his palm and adrenaline shot through his core.

Cyllus thrust up and clasped Savie's waist tight, holding her firm for the up and down motions. Through it all, he kept his mouth on hers, unwilling to lose the intimate connection.

She'd been right. Kissing bared the soul. It left an individual vulnerable but with that vulnerability came more. It filled him with the rich notes that all sang sweetly of Savie to his brain.

She broke from the kiss on a ragged moan. Passion lent her face a rosy glow as she trembled. Her lids rested at half-mast over drowsy blue eyes that gazed down at him and Cyllus was hooked. Hooked on Savie. No other could compare.

"Cyllus, Cy, what are we doing?"

"Do you want to stop?" he asked, stroking back the waves of her hair trailing about their faces.

"I think." She shook her head, blinking like a startled bird. "I don't know what to think."

As much as Cyllus desired Savie, he wouldn't do anything she wasn't ready for. "There is no rush."

Relief rolled across her face. She rubbed his shoulders, then folded her arms on his chest and rested her chin on her knuckles. "Was that as hot for you as it was for me?"

***

Beneath her, Cyllus' muscles flexed and rippled, the thick cock below pulsing against her thigh. Every minute move increased the arousal coursing through Savie's veins. They still wore their clothes, but several of the buttons on his shirt were missing. His pants gaped at the waist where she'd undone the zipper.

She fought the need to feel shame. Two years had gone by since she'd been with anyone sexually. Had abstinence made her desperate?

Her brain rejected the thought instantly. She was desperate but that wasn't the explanation for the desire and attraction that burned between her and Cyllus.

The golden brown eyes peering up at her contained shadows that hinted at secrets Savie wasn't sure she wanted to know. Their position lent a deeper sense of intimacy to this quiet space between them. Hoping to lighten the intensity of the moment, she went for humor. "Was that as hot for you as it was for me?"

His lips twitched and Savie's heart lifted for pulling the gesture from him. She had the feeling Cyllus hadn't had much to smile about lately. Whenever she was around him and his friends, they all seemed on edge. Maybe Savie could rescue him the way he'd rescued her. All she had to do was open her heart to him.

His thumb caressed the outer shell of her ear, sending goosebumps down her spine. She shivered uncontrollably, drawing a half-smile from him. "I'd venture to say it was better."

He meant it. Savie could have kissed him again in relief. As if in agreement, the firm length between her legs pulsed once more. She wasn't wearing underwear beneath her pants and dampness left her thighs coated with her slick essence. Savie needed to change the subject or she'd take what her body demanded. What it was clear Cyllus still wanted.

That wouldn't be wrong. Not exactly. She'd called a halt for a reason. Fear and strain were a poor recipe for sex. "What's next?"

Breath sighed from his full lips as he heaved upward, pulling Savie with him into an upright position. Her legs fell to the outside of his thighs, straddling him. She looped her arms about his neck loosely, comfortable in a way she'd never been with previous lovers.

"We're heading to Solus as we speak. Sora believes she might find a member of her pod there."

"Pod?" Savie didn't understand the term.

Cyllus grasped her hips and searched her face. Savie wanted to duck and avoid the probing look but she held firm and didn't break his gaze. Finally, he said, "Remember when I explained we're cyborgs?"

A fact which still blew Savie's mind. "Yes."

"When the transition process is complete, we're assigned pods. They usually consist of those converted under cybernetics at the same time. We're linked to that four or five individual grouping."

Savie dropped one hand from his neck to fiddle with the loose thread from a torn, missing button on his shirt. "Are those on this ship your pod people?"

The corner of Cyllus' lips curled, his body beneath her vibrating in amusement. "Just pod. Or our brethren. Only Kelix is from my pod. When judgment came down based on our alleged crimes, all cyborgs were separated and placed on various transport ships headed to Tyurma."

"What is Tyurma?" she stumbled over the strange word.

"A prison moon."

He'd really been convicted of a crime. The truth of it smacked Savie in the face and she could no longer ignore it. "I need to know, Cyllus. When you say you were guilty of the accusations, what did you do?"

Pain flashed over his face, putting the CR mark in stark contrast over his golden skin. "I'll understand if what I'm about to say changes your feelings about...this...us."

If Savie could promise she'd feel the same, she would, but a part of her didn't think she could handle something extreme and pretend. Not after all she'd gone through. "Tell me."

"Kirs is ruled by an emperor. He gave direction to our military to control a neighboring planet. Bionus. We, cyborgs and other members of the Military Elite, responded without question to quell what we thought was a potential danger to Kirs. It wasn't. It took time but gradually we realized Emperor Shui merely wanted to rule Bionus as well.

"At the time, the messages and orders we received conflicted but we ignored that. Then it came to our attention that we'd been misled. A rebellion grew among citizens, cyborgs and others. The emperor discovered we weren't blindly following his rule and had those still on his side tear through cities, terrorizing people and imprisoning them."

Savie took a deep breath. So far what he'd shared had happened thousands of times before in history. At least on Earth. She'd read about soldier guilt and its long term impact. "What was your part?"

He flinched and his gaze turned inward. "I reported information on resisters initially. Information that saw them punished. My pod and I stormed a city and set buildings on fire. It was after hours and no one was inside but they could have been! I want to excuse myself but there *is* no excuse."

With that, Cyllus lifted her from his lap and sat her on the side of the bed while he stood and moved himself far away from her. He pounded his fist into the wall and yelled. Twice more he shouted before he turned and slumped back onto it to bury his face in his hands.

"I could have killed innocent people and their blood would be on my head," he hoarsely whispered.

The thought clearly pained him. It was written on his face. Savie rose from the bed and went to him. She gripped one of his arms, the muscles taut below the shirt. He looked up. Such anguish. His eyes burned with remembered agony at what he'd done. "You didn't know, Cy."

He dropped his head, as if unable to meet her gaze. "My sister and mother were brought in, accused of being accomplices in the rebellion. They weren't. That didn't stop them from being put on a transport bound for prison. If they die, it *will* be my fault."

Chapter 14

Cyllus couldn't believe he'd told Savie the full truth of his past. She hadn't fled in fear. She hadn't accused him of being a monster. The heat of her touch burned through his shirt sleeve. Shame and misery threatened to swallow him. Only the look in Savie's eyes held the darkness at bay.

There was nothing in her gaze or expression to reflect an awareness of the danger he posed to her. It would be so easy to snap her frail neck now that she knew the truth. If he wanted who they were to remain a secret, she was no match for his cyborg enhanced strength. Not many were.

"I'm sorry you're carrying that burden. Is there a way to find out what happened to them?" Blue eyes gleamed with concern, reminding Cyllus that he'd cut off his own arm before harming a single strand of hair on Savie's head. If she chose to report them to authority figures, there was nothing he would do to stop her.

"I can't access my mainframe which would open me up to a vast array of communication and resources. To do so means exposing myself to Shui. In the beginning, we did in small increments. It's no longer wise or worth the risk. I'm sure there are watchers waiting for any cyborg to be careless."

"Will going to Solus help?"

Her care was obvious. Cyllus released the breath he'd unintentionally held and lowered his respiratory stats to bring his systems to a state of forced calm. "Sora might find those in her pod there. Our goal is to reconnect with families and friends who were separated and that's a start."

She paused, her eyes filling with dread. Nervous tension coiled through her frame. "Is that where we'll part? Are you planning to leave me on Solus to make my way to Earth on my own?"

"Never!" Cyllus grabbed her and nuzzled her temple to whisper against her soft skin. The sweet scent he'd grown accustomed to filled his nostrils. "Never. I wouldn't abandon you, Savie. I'll help you find your people. Make sure there is a way for you to be safely returned to Earth."

Even if it doomed his dream of them being together

"Alright." She took a deep breath and exhaled. "We're going to Solus and will take it one step at a time."

"Yes." Cyllus leaned away, keeping his hands about her curves. He wasn't ready to let her go. Not before he had to. "We should feed you again. Are you hungry?"

Her lips pursed. "I could eat."

Smiling, he said, "We have better supplies. No more hydrated packs. The replicator is fully stocked."

***

Savie moaned and wrapped her lips around the spoon to catch the last sweet taste of the dessert she'd consumed. "What's it called again?"

"*Bushére*. Spongy cake, sweet berries and crème baked together."

"Well, it's delicious." She lowered her spoon and eyed her empty plate. The cake was the last of the foreign dishes Cy had introduced her to. She'd especially loved the grilled meat that reminded her of steak, cut thinly and juicy in the middle.

She had no intention of asking what animal it came from. The vegetables had been crisp if a bit peppery.

The door to the kitchen area opened and Sora entered with long strides. Her pace didn't slow at their presence. She went to the cold storage and withdrew a beverage in a long cylinder container. The top fizzled as she twisted it open then proceeded to down the drink. When she finished, she wiped the back of her hand across her mouth to clear the drops of moisture and finally faced them.

"Will you be staying on Solus with us?"

Savie eyed Cy as she'd decided to call him.

"Not him. You," Sora said, joining them at the table and pulling out a chair to drop down on it.

Savie wasn't sure how to treat the woman. Sora's mannerisms were abrupt, her dislike obvious as she waited for Savie's response.

"I'm not sure what I'll do when we get there. Cy has promised to help look into a way to get me back to Earth without any of you getting into trouble."

"Is that what you want?" Sora leaned forward, her forearm on the table as she pressed Savie for an answer. She waved her hand negligibly between Savie and Cy. "I thought you two were a thing."

Savie glanced at Cy but he merely reclined back as far as his long legs would allow and arched a brow at Savie.

Savie inhaled then blew out a breath. "That's between us."

Sora snorted. "I'm trying to figure out if this attraction brewing between you will prevent you from telling everything you know. Ever since he listened to your recorded journals, Cyllus has been acting in a way that could jeopardize our lives."

Cy stiffened but still didn't intervene. Savie straightened in her seat and glared. "I'm not going to get any of you in trouble. That's not my intent."

"Intent and actuality can cross paths. I'm just asking for some warning in case we find someone from my pod group on Solus. I'd rather not have to kill y—"

Cy abruptly stood, causing the chair to tip over. He had his hand about Sora's throat before Savie could blink. Sora didn't resist. The smile she offered up was full of mockery as she finished her sentence.

"—and draw Cyllus' ire. Which as you can see is a very real possibility."

"You aren't killing her," Cy snarled, not releasing the woman.

Shrugging, Sora said, "One of us might have to if it means preserving our safety."

Cy snatched her from the seat on a growl. Sora whipped up an arm, breaking the hold. She stepped to the side and held out a warning hand when Cy surged toward her. "Stop! We don't have to fight, Cyllus."

"No one is going to touch Savie," he growled in a way that sent Savie's hair standing at her nape.

"Then you better make damn sure she understands the seriousness of the knowledge she holds."

Cy glared. "Her own life is in danger. Savie's situation is similar to ours. The Elusans left her people. That's not in line with what we know of them. Who's to say they won't return to finish off the one person who can reveal their actions which violated the rules of the Protectorate in that sector."

Savie flinched as the truth of his words hit her. She *was* in danger. Damn it. Why hadn't she considered that the Elusans could very well not want anyone to find out what they'd done?

"What's going on here?" Tagan entered with narrowed eyes, taking in Sora's and Cy's stance fraught with tension.

Sora eased her posture and sank back into her chair as if nothing had occurred. "Not much. Just saying aloud the things that needed to be said."

Tagan's green gaze shifted to Savie. "For a being from a world we've never heard of, you sure cause a lot of trouble."

"Hey!" Savie resented that remark.

Without waiting for her to defend herself, he went to the replicator on the counter and keyed in his meal selection. Once his food was done, he joined them at the table.

The arrangement was fine for two. A decent sized woman and one overly large man. She and Cyllus. Three muscled cyborgs and Savie equaled...a tight fit. She shifted her legs to the side to give them more space. Tagan sneered and dug into his meal.

Sora poked at the empty plates Savie and Cy had left. "Kelix sent me here to say we should arrive at Solus this evening instead of nightfall as we'd originally thought."

She shoved to her feet and left. Tagan made an inelegant sound and kept eating. Cy reached over and grasped Savie's hand. "Everything will be fine."

Despite her doubts, she believed him. With every minute spent in his presence, her heart was expanding and making room for Cyllus.

Chapter 15

When they arrived on Solus all was quiet. The ship landed in a transport station with only a handful of other vessels that Savie could see beneath the fluorescent lights lining the ceiling.

"There isn't a lot of otherworld travel here." Cy must have noted her searching glance.

They walked together in a group, Kelix leading the way to the housing secured for them in a district for visiting travelers. Or so Cy had told her.

"Is it always like this?" Savie questioned.

Cy peered down into her face, the hand he braced on her lower back a firm weight, guiding her along. "The two suns over Solus are too far away to provide more than a haze to the planet's surface. So it tends to look like this, maybe a little lighter at other times."

It was a marvel. Everywhere she looked there was technology far beyond any she'd ever witnessed. Earth had changed a lot if the history discs and holos were anything to go by. Primitive methods for food preparation and the drain on the planet's resources had required major work and adjustments.

As result, Savie always thought the tech and structures of new buildings filled with the digital advancements and automaton were the height of technology. Her experience with space travel and Algor 1 proved that wrong. Humans were far behind other species when it came to innovation.

Hell, the space travel alone was something they'd failed to achieve besides the infrequent moon explorations and unmanned rovers sent further out over the last centuries.

Cy and his friends were walking, talking signs of a technology Earth had yet to achieve.

"Are you okay?" Cy asked as they drew near a multi-floor building with a multitude of windows and twinkling lights.

His question brought something else to mind. "How do you know my language so well? When your friend Kelix talked to the transport station employee I could tell they spoke another language but I understood every word. I assumed it was because of my implant but you have a fine understanding of the nuances of my language."

Tagan grunted and came close to them, proving he'd been listening all along. "Didn't the Elusans explain anything to you? Or did you believe what you wanted?"

They hadn't. Not as much as she realized they should have. Behind Tagan's insensitive questions, she sensed his irritation. On her behalf. Shocking.

"Leave her be," Sora muttered from ahead.

Another surprise defense.

Reo had also drawn closer on her other side, a bare inch of space between his arm and hers. He didn't speak but Savie felt his tension bubbling under the surface just waiting for an outlet.

"Universal translator," Cy answered, unaware that Reo seemed one misstep away from exploding. "It's continually updated. As cyborgs, our processors also aid in language adaptations. Usually. We've learned not every cyborg grouping came out the same."

Reo had touched on that. Savie hadn't realized how complex the translators were. They stopped at the high rise building.

Using a magnetic key card, Kelix swiped them into the main lobby. "These are residential quarters. I have us all on the same floor and next to each other. Two to a room."

He passed around what looked like a narrow, thin chip the size of her pinky finger. Cy accepted one. "Savie and I are together."

Kelix rolled his eyes. "That was assumed. We'll regroup in the morning and follow up on the information regarding Sora's missing pod members."

They broke off, with Sora and Kelix taking the stairs under an arched doorway. Tagan and Reo went to a glass enclosure that rose swiftly and was soon out of sight.

"This way." Cyllus led her to another glass enclosure. "We're on the eleventh floor."

"Should we have taken the stairs?" Savie asked.

Facing the doors as the elevator rose, Cyllus asked, "Did you want to try eleven flights?"

Not even.

Savie pressed her lips together and pretended to miss Cyllus' smug smile. He was right and she wasn't going to argue needlessly.

Cy showed her around the suite with its basic décor and functional furniture. "If there's anything you want or need, feel free to ask and I'll make sure you have it."

He moved away and went to a wall-mounted screen. Savie took a moment to check things out in more detail. She began opening doors in search of the bathroom. One held empty shelves. Another opened into an empty closet with tiled walls and square inserts.

"The cleansing unit." Cy spoke over her shoulder.

Savie glanced at him. "Can you turn it on for me? I desperately want a shower."

"Of course, Savie." He stretched an arm out, his skin brushing the side of her throat. With a wave of his hand, water sprayed from the ceiling.

She stared in awe at the tiny slits creating the waterfall effect.

"These are the temperature gauges." Cy pointed at the square plates inserted at the halfway mark of the wall in front of her. "This one controls the spray pressure."

He demonstrated by tapping an insert.

"Got it."

When he moved back, she realized she'd have to undress here in the living room area. Not quite the bathroom she'd been expecting. "What if I have to—"

"Over here," he cut off, showing her the door right next to the shower closet.

"Thanks." Savie managed a smile which quivered at the corners. It wasn't that she was tired or shy. Well, maybe shy, but desire had returned and she hoped the shower would cool her off.

Quickly, she tossed the shirt over her head, removed her pants, socks and boots then stepped into the narrow space. Pulling the door closed behind her, she had to fight the feeling of claustrophobia. This was tight. Now inside, she did notice a nook for clothing or towels.

She adjusted the water to just below steaming hot and discovered a switch that poured pink foam in her hand similar to what she'd used on the ship.

Fifteen minutes later, Savie came out and paused.

"Here." Cy walked toward her, holding up a large green thick cloth. She accepted it and dried off, looping the fabric about her torso and knotting it to stay in place.

"I have one of my shirts on the bed in the other room for you to use. I can sleep out here if it bothers you."

Leaving her to sleep alone. The thought shot a jolt of discomfort down her spine. Savie didn't want to be alone. Especially not at night when her dark grief returned. "No. I'm used to sharing the bed with you."

Cy snagged her around the waist and pulled her in close. "You don't have to be scared anymore, Savie. I promised I'd help you and my assistance doesn't come with a price."

She knew that. His every action since he'd taken her from the domed labs on Algor 1 had been mindful of her care.

Sighing, she leaned up and kissed the corner of his jaw. "I know. I can't possibly thank you, Cy."

"You already have. By surviving. Hanging on until I was able to get to you."

Savie had never had someone display such a deep level of commitment toward her before. She bit her lip then asked, "My team—"

Cy stopped the words with a finger to her mouth. "I'll find away to ensure they are returned home respectfully."

They made their way to the bedroom, Cy undressing with an efficiency and grace she envied. Savie spotted the large shirt he'd left for her and dropped it over her head.

His scent rose from the collar and surrounded her just like when she was in his arms. She climbed into the bed and pulled the covers over her. A moment later, the side of the thick mattress depressed as Cy joined her. She caught a glimpse of his pants.

Maybe he didn't trust himself fully.

"Lights out," Cy said.

Darkness engulfed the room at his command. Settling down further under the covers, Savie didn't resist when Cy entwined his body about hers. An arm banded around her waist and her head landed on his shoulder. Perfectly innocent.

"Sleep. Tomorrow will be a new day," he whispered.

Savie tried. She really did but her body hummed with energy and disquiet. Cy's chest rose and fell beneath her cheek, his heartbeat a reassuring thrum in her ears. Cautiously she slid one of her legs between his. He absently adjusted, making room and resting his head on top of hers.

Sleep had come easily to him. Meanwhile Savie's mind was going a hundred miles an hour. It didn't help that her nipples were hard nubs beneath the shirt he'd given her.

Savie shifted on her side, hoping a change of position would help. This only pressed their lower halves in closer proximity. He might be happily asleep but his cock wasn't. The large bulge nestled between her thighs and flexed.

Savie bit off a moan and stared into the dark. She could just make out the outline of his upper shoulder, the curve of his collarbone and the profile of his face.

He was a kind man. He might not think he was but Savie knew it to be so. Rescuing her, helping his friends and maintaining his own determined search for his family were all signs of his character.

He was also ridiculously attractive. She'd have to be a fool to pretend his looks weren't eye-catching. A body rippling with corded muscles would draw any eye, definitely hers. Unable to resist, she pressed her lips to the bare skin of his chest.

He flinched but didn't wake. Tentatively and with an eye on his face to see if he woke, Savie licked the smooth skin. The same scent his clothes carried burst on her tongue as a flavor. Heavy oak and musk with spices rolled all in one.

She couldn't hold back her next moan and pressed her thigh closer between his, rubbing against his thickening cock. Rocking her hips against the solid bulge, Savie trailed kisses across his chest, grazed her teeth over the tiny bump of his nipple and closed her eyes as sensations cascaded over her.

Fire. Her body was on fire and all she wanted was to burn alive in the passionate flames he brought out in her. Lowering a hand to the waist of his pants, she sought his erection. Her palm filled with the curved length and she stroked in pleasure.

Firm fingers dove into her hair, holding her head in place. Savie froze.

"I thought we agreed we weren't going to do this," Cy mumbled in a sleep roughened voice.

His statement brought Savie back to her senses but she didn't release him. If anything, the hand on his thick cock continued to stroke up and down. Hunger exploded through her body and she nipped, bit, and clawed at him, pushing until Cy rolled onto his back with her on top.

"Savie. Savannah. It's okay," Cy whispered. "Use me if you want."

That was exactly it. She wanted to use him, feel the passion seething between them come to life and wash all her doubts and thoughts away.

And more than anything Savie wanted to feel alive. With a fierce growl, she rose and mashed her lips to Cy's, kissing him with pent up frustration.

His hands clamped down on her hips and he moved her body up and down, his hips following in counterpoint.

Satisfaction. It was what she wanted. Crying out and pleading for him to fill her, Savie buried her hands in Cy's hair. "I want you. Right now."

"Then you can have me."

His hands fell from her waist as he pulled and tugged until he got his pants to his knees. Savie scrambled up and helped until he was able to kick them off. The covers tangled about them and she shoved them off impatiently.

His body lay bare before her and she took only a moment to enjoy the visual then tore of the shirt he'd loaned her. She dove over him, reclaiming her spot on top of him, hip to hip, the erotic thrust of his cock nudging at her damp and dripping folds.

Chapter 16

Cyllus had awakened from one breath to the next aroused beyond belief. Finding Savie taking her pleasure of him had only increased his rampant desire. Propped over him with her legs straddling his hips, she was his perfect fantasy.

Plump breasts swayed, the color of her nipples indeterminable in the darkness even with his enhanced vision. None of that mattered, though. Her fat nubs teased like a succulent dessert. Cy stroked his hands up her torso, tested the weight of her breasts and squeezed.

Another soft cry fell from her lips. "Cy, I want you."

She rocked on his lap and he met each downward slant with an upward pump. Wetness coated his groin, his cock slick with her moisture as he slid between her plump lower lips.

"You have me, Savie. I'm not going anywhere.

She locked her legs about him as if afraid he'd move away. He wouldn't dream of leaving this bed. Not when he finally had what he craved filling his palms.

His thumbs plucked at her nipples on that thought and Savie arched on a hiss, her hands digging into his shoulders.

"Take me. Take what you want." He needed to know Savie wanted him as much as he wanted her.

"Wait. Need...you." Savie rose on her haunches.

At first, Cy thought she'd changed her mind. His head fell back on the pillow and he groaned. Then her fingers were on him again, clasping his erection in a firm grip as she stroked then guided him to her entrance.

"Fuuuck," Cy groaned and helped. His hand covered hers and together they worked back and forth until his head penetrated.

She sucked him in and he slid another few inches, stroking and gliding through the tight wetness. And warmth. Here was the heat Cy hadn't allowed himself in years.

"I have a birth control implant and inoculations against most sexual diseases," she whispered.

"Same. As a cyborg my nanobots would also filter any infection in my body."

Her smile was full of wicked pleasure. "Good."

Cy was no longer cold with Savie in his arms. He wrapped his arms around her back and pulled her in close to mutter, "Gotta be deep. Want to feel you."

"Yes. Fuck me hard and deep, Cy."

Her words, the drugged quality to them, matched the fever burning inside of him. Cy flipped them over, balancing his weight on his forearms as he loomed over Savie. They were still connected but the change in position slid him in so deep his every muscle clenched and he had to grit his teeth to keep from coming.

"Feels good. You feel so good, Savie," he panted once he felt in control.

"Please don't stop." Savie undulated beneath him, her hands hooked over his shoulder as she used him as a brace to rise up and down on his cock from below.

Forget control. There was no control. Cy pounded into her, letting each thrust and her grip on his cock fuel him. Grunts fell from his lips, hoarse sounds he couldn't hold in. Savie matched him vocally with cries, moans and toward the end, a scream that blasted his auditory circuits.

She'd done that before—shorted his hearing with her screams when they'd been racing from her domed lab. Now the sound was a precursor to her orgasm. Cy drove his hips forward again, caught one leg under the knee and lifted it higher.

Her nails raked his back, tiny stings setting his muscles to twitching.

"Yes, yes, yes," she said. "I'm going to come."

A little bit more. She only needed a little bit more. Cy lowered his head and kissed the smooth line of her arched throat. He licked the pulsing vein along the side and sucked, knowing he'd leave a bruise in the morning.

He didn't care. Cy couldn't care about anything with his mind caught up in the whirlwind that was Savie. He fisted her hair and growled, "Now, Savie. Come now, baby."

Savie screamed again and clamped down like a vise on his plunging cock as she climaxed. Cy's orgasm slammed into him with the force of a freighter. Her internal muscles continued to flutter and work his length.

"Fuck, fuck," he gasped, falling forward.

He caught himself before he crushed her and collapsed to the side of her, his face flat in the pillow. He couldn't lift his head. His heart raced, his senses alive and firing. His processors tried to counteract the rush of adrenaline but Cy shut it down, wanting to absorb it all without artificial interference.

When minutes had ticked by, he drew in a ragged breath. Savie's hands smoothed up his spine before falling to the bed. He tipped his head up and her exhausted smile, teeth gleaming, eased his tension.

"I take it you couldn't sleep." As an opening statement after what they'd shared, Cy admitted it wasn't his best. He needed more time to gather his thoughts.

Savie chuckled weakly and patted the bed. "Hold me."

Laughing, Cy gathered her in his arms and placed her in front of him, resuming their previous sleeping position. His leg slid between hers, his thigh instantly saturated by their mixed fluids leaking out. Savie ran her hand up and down his forearm at her waist. "I'm sorry."

His heart stuttered. Did she regret what happened? Was he mistaken in thinking she was awake and aware?

"Sorry for what?" he asked calmly while his pulse kicked up.

"For taking advantage of you when you were trying to sleep."

Breath sawed from him. "Feel free to wake me like that any time, Savie. I'm yours."

He was. He belonged to Savannah Monroe. He'd been living in a cold state, simply existing, following commands. There had been no joy, no happiness outside the few moments he spent with his mother and sister and even those were fleeting at best as he started avoiding them for fear he'd lose the last connection left to him.

Savie's journals had brought him back to life. His arm tightened around her and he placed his chin on her shoulder. Her wild hair tumbled about their faces but he didn't care. The scent of sex filled the room with its cloying thickness and Cy stored it in his memory banks to recall at will when she left him.

Cy smiled and palmed the smooth skin of her lower stomach. His thumb caressed the indentation caused by her belly button and she shivered as the tips of his fingers touched the silk hair of her mound. He wished the lights had been on. Next time he'd spend more time appreciating Savie's body—worshipping it appropriately as he brought her to release over and over again.

In the morning, he'd—a light snore snagged his attention. "Savie?"

She hummed under her breath and burrowed deeper into the bed. She was asleep. Cy eased his arm from around her and rose from the bed to find the covers. He tucked her in and considered lying back beside her.

Except now that he was awake, he had work to do.

Once assured she slept, he tugged on his wrinkled pants and went into the main room. Grimacing at the sight of the basic comp unit built onto the wall, he accepted it was all he had to work with right now. There was no point in being frustrated at knowing he contained a faster, more efficient mainframe and system right in his own head yet couldn't use it.

The next nights were an effort in diligence. Once Cy committed to his mission, he was relentless. He scoured records and databases for any and all information on Earth. He dealt with the slow system and the outdated tech despite hitting frustrating road blocks time and again. Cy had made a promise and planned to uphold it.

It took three days. Three days in which his mornings were spent making love to Savie and his nights were spent searching for information on her world and its connection with the Vassi.

Now, on the fourth night, as he sat in front of the comp with a name and contact information, joy at his success alluded him. Savie lay in the bed they shared, unaware of what he'd been working on and now he had to decide how to tell her what he'd discovered.

Would she want to leave right away?

Despite knowing this would eventually happen, Cy still found himself unprepared for the onslaught of emotions at the idea of Savie leaving. Sleeping together and becoming sexually involved had only made his addiction for her stronger.

He didn't want her to return to Earth. But what did he have to offer? A life on the run, branded as an accessory to a criminal? In addition, life onboard a ship would be hard. Unless they stayed on Solus.

His mind latched on to the idea. It could work. They'd still have to be careful and constantly stay on guard but maybe, just maybe, Savie wouldn't mind.

"Open the door. I have news," Kelix said across his NNP.

"I do as well," Cy responded, turning from the comp screen and heading for the door.

On the other side, Kelix stood beside a pale Sora. The cyborg female tended to be hard to read when she wasn't angry. While Cy searched for a way to get Savie safely home, Sora was dedicated to pursuing the lead from the Reapers to find her pod brethren here on Solus.

Each failure had seen her grow more and more drawn as she spent her nights scouring the streets and tracking any potential rumors or leads.

"We've got the location of a possible member from Sora's pod. No idea which one," Kelix said as soon as he faced Cy.

Sora tucked her hands under her armpits and shot him a look from beneath lowered brows. "Reo's already asleep. Are you coming?"

Cy glanced back in the direction of the bedroom where Savie slept.

"Tagan can stay and watch over her." Sora huffed and rolled her eyes. "I'd rather have you accompany us than him since you're more sensible."

Just then, Tagan shouldered his way between the two, not showing any reaction to Sora's insult. Cy hesitated a moment longer, the need to stay near Savie a pull he found it hard to fight. Especially in light of the fact she would be leaving him soon.

It was Kelix who pushed the decision. "Cy, we need you."

"Fine." Kelix rarely asked for anything. Turning to Tagan, who'd settled on the sofa, Cy warned, "Don't wake her. Don't scare her. In fact, don't say anything to her."

Tagan stared in disbelief then curled his lip. "Get out of here. The sooner you finish, the sooner you can return and not worry I'll scare your frail humanoid."

Cy growled but Kelix grabbed his arm. "Not now. We need to go."

Giving in, Cy spun and followed them. According to what Sora had discovered, someone had admitted to housing a strange man in their home. They wouldn't speak on it and the source said the person clammed up instantly when he tried to dig deeper.

All Sora had was an address to follow up on.

"You trust this?" Cy asked Sora.

Her eyes turned silver in eagerness. "I need to know regardless if it's the truth or not. I won't know unless I check it out."

Cy understood that. His pace slowed. He'd left the bulk of the work finding Xion and Kaito to Kelix. Tracking if his family still lived had fallen to the way side. Cy had been remiss in his duties because of his obsession with Savie. Another con in the column of why he didn't deserve someone to care for. There was too much going on in his life right now.

Kelix bumped his shoulder and gave a what the fuck look. Sighing, Cy sped up and didn't fall behind again.

The directions led them to a single-level house on the outskirts of a town less than eight kilometers away from the city where they'd secured their housing. It was evident the area struggled financially but each home had flowers in the front and the walkways were clean and appeared meticulously kept.

"This is it," Sora announced.

Chapter 17

Worry and nerves etched groove lines in Sora's cheeks and she wasn't maintaining her typical stoic expression. Hope burned like a blaze in her eyes as she pinned her gaze to the home before them.

"This is it. The address I was given," she said then pounded on the door hard enough to wake the dead.

Kelix and Cy stood guard and watched her back. Night cast everything in shadow and no one was out.

The door opened with a creak. The woman hovered at the jamb as she nervously eyed their large frames. Her blonde hair was worn in a messy ball at the top of her head. "Yes?"

Sora took a deep breath and Cy worried she'd ruin it by forcing her way inside. Instead, using the softest tone he'd ever heard from her, she said, "We're here about the stranger with the brand on his face."

The woman's eyes widened and she went to close the door on them. Sora caught the edge and kept a sliver open. Her voice dropped into a low growl. "You don't want to do that."

The blonde chewed her bottom lip until it gleamed a bright red. "I don't know what you're talking about. It's late, you should go."

Once more she attempted to close the door but Sora wasn't letting that happen. The stranger was no match for a cyborg.

"Please," Sora implored. "If you know his whereabouts, I need to find him."

"Who are you?" the lady finally asked, glancing anxiously over her shoulder into the interior of her home.

It was clear she didn't want them inside. Was she holding the cyborg prisoner? Doubtful. She wouldn't be able to match one in sheer strength. Then again, if the cyborg had been incapacitated, there was no telling what could have happened.

"My name's Sora and I've been searching for my missing friends."

"Sora?" The woman's tone changed, grew less cautious. Seconds later an outdoor light flicked on, throwing their faces in stark relief under the halogen glare.

The woman's gaze immediately went to the letters on Sora's cheek. Resolution and relief flashed. She leaned back and opened the door wider. "Come in."

They hurried inside and she slammed the door and hit the locking mechanism.

"Back here."

There were a total of four life forms inside the dwelling. Kelix dropped a hand to hover over his weapon and Cy did the same. Sora nodded at their reaction but didn't go for the laser belted at her hip.

They followed the woman down a short hall. It was a strategic nightmare and required them to walk single file. Cy tensed, the quiet putting him on guard in case they were walking into a trap. The threadbare furnishings he'd caught sight of spoke of an impoverished family. All the more likely this could be a way to lure them in.

At the end of the hall in the small confines of a back room, a large male lay on a pallet of blankets on the floor. His body was uncovered and completely nude. As they drew closer, Sora shoved a fist in her mouth and sank to her haunches beside his legs.

"Thalen," she choked out.

The dim lighting would have made it difficult to see if Cy had ordinary vision but he'd left ordinary behind the day he joined the military. Once he stepped all the way into the room, Cy froze. Twisted scarring and swollen red welts marked every inch of the man on the floor.

Diagnostic scans confirmed burns to seventy percent of his body. The reason he hadn't awakened had to be because he'd placed himself in repair mode and shut his systems down to conserve strength. This much damage would have been beyond his nanobots. No wonder he hadn't moved when they came in.

If he'd been awake and aware, the pain would be excruciating. The woman standing guard over his body watched them with cautious eyes.

"How long has he been like this?" Kelix asked in a hushed whisper.

"From the beginning," she said.

Sora crept closer and pointed out the rectangular box clenched tightly between the fingers of Thalen's right hand. White and blue streams arced in a dazzling display of electricity above the skin from wrist to forearm. "What's this?"

"Before he passed out, he claimed to be a cyborg from a far away world and said his nanobots wouldn't be enough. He begged me to find a power source. This is the backup mobile generator we use for the electric output to the house during bad storms. He ripped the backing off and gripped it in his bare hand then told me not to try and remove it. No matter what."

One touch from the raw energy Thalen was consuming in a continuous loop would have blown the woman apart instantly. It was the risky act of a desperate man. Thalen was smart. He'd found a way to give his body what it needed to aid in his recovery.

Still, for him to be out since the events on the transport signaled severe injuries beyond the surface ones they could see. Internal damage to this extent should have killed the cyborg but somehow he'd hung on.

"I hope that was okay," the woman continued. She glanced at Thalen in pity then to Sora with curiosity though she didn't ask any questions.

"You did good," Sora answered, staring at her fallen comrade. Her fingers caressed his wrist, making sure not to dislodge his hold on the power box. Tiny darts of energy flickered and bounced from her fingers then back to Thalen.

The phenom reminded him of her odd ability on the transport that had disrupted the energy field and enabled them to escape their cell. Then on the machine to issue them money.

Sadness reflected in her gaze and Cy was sure they weren't meant to witness the emotion. Was this just a pod brethren or did he mean more to her?

Sora turned her gaze up to them. "He can't be moved yet. We should head back."

She rose to her feet and walked out without a backward glance. Shock gave way to confusion. Cy exchanged a worried glance with Kelix, who shrugged and pulled out one of the debit cards Sora had stolen for them at the bazaar on Dianides.

"Let us pay you for the care you've given him and any necessities you may need while he recovers."

She wanted to refuse. The protest on the edge of her trembling lips but it was clear she'd hit hard times. It would have been easy to ignore a stranger in need yet she'd not only taken him in her home, she'd cared for him and kept his presence hidden.

Until she'd let slip a minor detail to a perceived friend who'd spoken to one of Sora's contacts.

Cy's scanners picked up sleeping life forms in the adjoining room. Three. Based on the woman's exhausted demeanor and the tiny toy she hadn't quite managed to kick under a chair when they entered, he surmised she had kids to look after.

"Sure." She rushed across the room and came back with a card reader. Kelix paid and slid the card back in his pocket. "Our thanks. We'll be in touch."

He left and Cy paused. He debated his next words then went with his gut. "Your friend you told isn't trustworthy. I'd be mindful of anything I told them in the future."

Disappointment pinched her lips tight but she offered him a clipped nod.

Cy found his way out and joined Sora and Kelix for their return.

***

Savie awoke alone in the bed. She ran her hand over the sheets behind her. Cool to the touch. Cy had gotten up long enough for his body heat to have faded from the linen. She blinked against the sliver of light which was all the two suns shining through the window gave off during the day. She tried to place the time.

Had to be morning. Another day in which she needed to figure out what her future plans were. Voices from the outer room drew her attention. Cy and another masculine tone.

Planning to announce her presence before going to shower and dress, she heard her name.

Savie stopped at the door and listened at the crack.

"You haven't let me down."

That was Kelix. Savie would recognize his brusque voice anywhere.

"So much of my attention has been spent on Savie and you were right to call me on it," Cy said.

Savie flinched. Did Kelix have a problem with Savie and Cy being together? It was obvious he wasn't fond of her and he didn't go out of his way to speak to her. Then again, none of them did. They seemed fully focused on finding other cyborgs from Kirs. Could she blame them?

"That doesn't mean you let me down. The question is, what do you plan to do about her now?"

"I'm meeting with the Andruvion. Depending on what he says, it shouldn't take long to make arrangements for her to go home."

Go home. He meant her. Savie jerked back from the door as her heart split down the center. A rush of disappointment filled her. Granted, he'd told her he would help her find a way back to Earth but after the last few days, she'd thought there was something between them. Something stronger than rescuer and helpless victim.

Had she been mistaken?

The voices rumbled on but she was too dazed to keep listening. All she heard was Cy's voice saying he was sending her back. Didn't she deserve a say in what happened to her?

That quickly anger came to her aid. Savie knotted her hands at her side. How dare he?! This was supposed to be something he discussed with her not with his friend.

Pushing the bedroom door open, she stalked into the living area prepared to blast him. Kelix and Cy shifted to glance in her direction. Banging on the exterior door interrupted her. Sora, Tagan and Reo entered without waiting for permission.

Cy didn't seem startled. "Glad you're here."

They formed a circle and resumed talking in low whispers there was no way she could hear. Savie folded her arms across her middle, unable to believe Cy hadn't greeted her with his husky good morning and kiss to the temple she'd grown accustomed to.

Heart sick, she let her hands fall slack at her side. Staring a moment longer to see if he'd speak to her, she finally turned away, grabbed her clothes and went into the tiny confines of the shower closet.

As she lathered up with the foam cleanser, Savie was glad she hadn't confronted Cy. It would have only made her look like a fool.

Chapter 18

Showered and dressed in one of the few outfits Cy purchased for her, Savie entered the living room. Only Sora and Tagan remained.

Seeing her glance around, Sora rose from the seat she'd taken. "Cyllus went with Kelix to look into something for you. Tagan and I can take you to him if you'd like."

Savie considered it for all of two seconds, then pasted a bright fake smile on her face. "Actually, I'd like to go out. I've been stuck inside since we got here."

"Because we're wanted." Tagan jabbed a finger at the brand on his face. "This is called laying low."

Sora scowled before turning back to Savie. "We can go out. I can't imagine how you feel. I'd go crazy trapped in these four walls."

"Thank you."

"Consider me out." Tagan stood and sent them both a mocking salute. "I want no parts of Cyllus tearing me limb from limb when he finds out she left the building."

With that, he walked to the door and left.

Sora snorted. "Like you need permission."

It was unexpected support and the grin that stretched Savie's face was far more genuine. "I'm ready when you are."

They took the elevator to the lower level. In the lobby, the ebb and flow of pedestrian traffic was higher than when she'd arrived a few days ago. It also gave Savie her first true taste of various aliens. Yes, she knew the Vassi looked like a cross between two popular movie aliens from old vids.

She'd only seen them on screen via The Hive social network, though. The Elusans had glowing outlines for bodies that had taken some getting used to but no facial features to attach unusual characteristics.

Savie couldn't really count Cy and the other cyborgs as truly alien either since they bared a strong resemblance to humans.

In the lobby, everyone they passed had pale blue or lavender skin. Antenna on their heads wobbled left and right. They didn't have lips. Instead, thin slits opened and closed as they spoke animatedly.

And Savie understood every word she caught. Simply amazing.

"There's a place not far in walking distance where we can grab food and drink."

Sora's suggestion agreed with her stomach, which chose that moment to gurgle. The sound brought a smile to the usually taciturn cyborg.

Before they reached the door to exit, a tall silhouette joined them, stilling Savie in her tracks. Sora didn't seem surprised. "If you're coming, don't get in the way."

Reo inclined his head but waited until Savie had gone through the door before following. He seemed content to join them, walking a few steps behind. Sora waggled her brows at Savie and shrugged.

Savie remembered Cy saying Reo had lost his pod members. Perhaps that was why he came across as morose and adrift.

There was a star chart on the wall of the eatery Sora took her to. Savie didn't recognize any of it. Then again, she'd seen a star chart back on Earth years ago and outside the planets in her solar system she'd learned as a child, none of it was remotely familiar.

Cy had taken one look at the chart in their room and seemed to know where they were and where they'd come from when he rescued her. He'd chatted on and on assuming she understood. Savie hadn't.

Maybe it was a cyborg thing but she didn't think so. Alien beings use to traveling among the stars probably had things like various star charts memorized. An advanced version of GPS for people who had a better grasp of how things were supposed to look as opposed to humans who'd never established life off of Earth.

Hell, they'd never traveled beyond the moon and sending unmanned rovers to other planets didn't count. She and Lexie had joked about that during their trip on the Elusans ship. Lexie, who wouldn't get the chance to learn about star charts.

After this experience, Savie made a vow to better understand space and the travel involved going forward. She'd do it as a small way to honor her friend.

If the Vassi didn't punish her or have the United Territories charge her with a crime, Savie hoped to space travel again. The right way, with all proper papers submitted that said she could leave Earth and not fear for her life.

That could take months, though. Maybe years. In that time, would Cy find someone else? What if he fell in love?

Her breath seized and she worked to draw air in her lungs. She exhaled on an explosion of sound. It wasn't much she could do to change things. He'd made his feelings known by planning to send her back without talking to her first.

"Savie, are you alright?" Sora reached over and lightly touched her hand.

"W-what?" Savie startled and realized she'd followed them blindly to a table.

"You seemed lost in thought," Sora said, sitting at the circular table on an outside paved veranda.

There were only two wrought iron chairs contoured for comfort and with a thick tan cushion on the bottom. Reo propped himself on the column between the next table and theirs, leaving the remaining chair for Savie.

Other customers and staff took a wide berth around him. Savie couldn't blame them. He was a large man whose body was clearly defined with muscle in the black shirt and pants he wore. His thick soled boots looked like he stomped on people for fun.

For his part, Reo's behavior didn't exactly help. He appeared as if he didn't give two shakes about how people regarded him. While his expression remained neutral, an air of danger flowed from him. His gaze constantly scanned around them as if he expected trouble lurking at every corner. The other diners were wise to steer clear of him.

Pressing buttons on a table, Sora said, "Here are some things I think you might like."

A holo screen opened in the middle of the table and displayed several colorful dishes. Savie looked at the descriptions flowing in script beneath each revolving item as it floated above the page and chuckled. "I can't read any of this."

The translator might have helped her understand and speak most languages but she couldn't read the squiggles at all.

"Huh. I didn't think of that. Well, this is..." Sora proceeded to go over what the four dishes contained. "As someone with a palate unaccustomed to foreign food, these options are safe."

"Okay. I'll have all the things you suggested."

Behind them, Reo snorted in what could have been a laugh, but when Savie glanced over her shoulder, he was back to staring off into the distance.

After placing their order, Sora leaned over the table and lowered her voice. "Why do you think Reo wanted to come along?"

Savie frowned. She had no idea. The cyborg had been kind for lack of a better word with a side of neutral thrown in after their conversation when they were alone on the ship. She shrugged. "Maybe he needed to get out."

When Sora pursed her lips in disbelief, Savie rushed to redirect the conversation, sensing Reo was paying more attention to them than he let on.

"Cy said you had information on one of your...pod. Did you find them?"

Waiting until after their plates were set before them, Sora spoke as she dug into the savory dishes. "Thalen. Yes. In fact, we ventured out a few nights ago to see if he was here."

Intrigued, Savie asked, "And?"

"He was." Sora paused in her meal to meet Savie's gaze. The steely gray glint was softer than Savie had ever witnessed. "He's been injured badly but I found him."

"Is he someone special to you?" Savie asked delicately, wondering if this Thalen was more than a friend.

Sora finished her food and pushed the empty plate away. "He's my best friend. Almost like a brother. We grew up together on Kirs. Played and fought. When it came time to make adult choices, we decided to join the military at the same time and later made the decision to become cyborgs together."

Hollowed shadows were dug deep beneath Sora's eyes.

"You have no idea what a relief it is to find him alive. I want to find my other pod members too but this, Thalen...it was important and means a lot that I found him first."

Sora blinked away tears and cleared her throat. Reo spoke up. "You are lucky. I wouldn't wish my situation on another."

Savie glanced at him and the depth of pain glimmering in Reo's magnetic gaze was like a blow to the gut. There would be no relief for him. His pod was dead. For the first time, Savie felt like she was truly seeing the suffering the cyborgs' had to deal with.

Cy had to be experiencing this same degree of pain and doubt but he'd managed to find information about Earth. For Savie. She shouldn't have gotten angry this morning when it was clear he understood being adrift and away from family and friends more than anyone else.

He was trying to prevent her from going through what he was going through. She'd thought Cy went behind her back to betray her when he'd actually helped her. The sense of devastation hearing his words earlier had her near tears. That's what she got for reacting with her heart and not her mind.

His mother's and sister's fate were unknown and he still had two men from his pod missing, yet he worked to ensure Savie could go back home. The feeling growing inside solidified into a painful knot in her stomach. She needed to return and talk to him.

Shoving her chair back, Savie surged to her feet and bumped into someone behind her.

"Watch it!" a voice roared.

Savie flinched and turned to apologize. "I'm sorry."

Standing before her was an alien, a living, breathing scary alien. He didn't favor the ones with antenna, who nodded and smiled in passing at her. Instead, this man towered over her, his massive chest taking up her entire view. Wild red hair tangled about craggy features set in a face of dark blue scales. Claws clicked on the ends of his long fingers. Savie took a half-step back.

He stepped forward, brawny arms flexing in the sleeveless vest and leaned toward her with his intimidating presence. "You need to watch yourself."

"Move away from me," Reo growled from somewhere behind her.

Savie swallowed and held the blue alien's gaze. She didn't dare look away. "I'm really sorry."

There were three others with the shaggy haired man. Scaled aliens with wild hair and claws too.

"What are you?!" The first alien's nostrils flared as if her smell offended him.

Not sure if she should share that information, Savie glanced toward Sora who pushed back customers blocking her from reaching Savie.

"I'm talking to you!" he roared and grabbed Savie around the shoulders, fingers digging cruelly through her shirt.

She strained and twisted but his harsh hold was solid, lifting her onto her toes. Suddenly Reo was at Savie's side. He wrenched her attacker's fingers back, freeing Savie and shoved her attacker away, snarling, "Fuck off!"

She'd barely caught her breath when Reo pulled Savie into the protective curve of his shoulders. Her attackers' friends all shouted at once. "Leave her alone, Kjar!"

Other customers leaped to their feet, running from the commotion. Someone slammed into Savie's side and she felt herself slipping. Reo caught her arm then pushed her behind him with a hand locked about her waist.

"Move out of the way. I'll teach her not to push anyone." Kjar reached for Savie, his intent to crush Reo in the process evident.

A cold knot twisted in Savie's gut. Her heart leaped and her pulse went wild. Sora slid into position in front of Reo and Savie. "You don't want to go there."

The words were uttered in the coldest tone, Savie had ever heard Sora use.

Too bad, Kjar didn't heed the warning. His swung his beefy fist with deadly intent. Savie knew if it connected he'd crush Sora's entire skull. Reo stiffened but his arm held Savie locked in place directly behind him.

Sora caught the giant's wrist hovering in the air and twisted. The sound he made was a cross between a bark and a howl of pain. Not wasting time, Sora raised her leg and kicked hard. The force sent Kjar flying across the floor. Along the way, he crashed over several chairs.

Cringing, Savie clutched the back of Reo's shirt. She caught Sora's gaze and the other woman winked. Actually winked.

Savie edged backward, using her grip on Reo's shirt to try and move him with her. It was like attempting to move a two ton vehicle. He didn't budge, didn't even give Savie the courtesy of a glance over his shoulder.

Staggering to his feet, Kjar flipped over the table near him, dishes clattering to the floor. Staff hurried over to see what was going on. Shouts and arguing ensued. Kjar's friends tried to calm things and get in between him and the cyborgs.

Kjar snatched them up by their shirts and flung them to the side.

"Oh, shit," Savie muttered, eyes wide at the behemoth who leaned forward and charged.

Sora planted a foot, pivoted on her hip and punched him right in the face. He went down instantly. The crowd's reaction was a low sympathetic moan.

Shaking off the pain, Kjar shot a look at his friends who rushed to his side. Waving off their help, he shouted, "Ophom, Yaheen, don't just watch. Get them!"

After a brief hesitation, Ophom and Yaheen turned toward them. Reo moved Savie farther away.

"Stay back. Don't get in the way," he cautioned, gaze on the two men rushing forward.

Sora signaled to Reo and they split their focus, Sora went for Ophom and Reo took on Yaheen.

Sora fought with brutal cruel intensity. Her kicks and punches were aimed to take her opponent down. Reo's style was the opposite. Lip curled, he bared his teeth and goaded Yaheen.

Taking the bait, Yaheen lunged for Reo, a punch meant for his face. Reo ducked, swiveled about and slammed his fist in Yaheen's gut. Yaheen gagged and tried to dodge away but Reo caught him by the throat then tossed him with full force into the wall behind him. Yaheen slid to the floor and didn't get back up.

"Youuuu!" Back on his feet, Kjar locked eyes with Savie from her place against the wall. She only had time to grab an overturned chair. As he neared, she reared back with both hands tight to the framing and swung.

The chair cracked over his scaly face, shattering on contact. It barely slowed him down. Savie squeaked as Kjar lunged. Reo caught him from behind and kicked. Kjar folded. Gripping his knee, he screamed in pain. Reo leaned over and reached out as if to offer aid.

Breathing roughly, Kjar looked up. His eyes reddened. Reo palmed the injured knee and squeezed. The cracking sound of bone breaking had Savie wincing. Kjar screamed in agony.

"You should have accepted her apology." Reo stepped over the sprawled man and placed a guiding hand on Savie's shoulder. He turned her toward the door to leave.

Sora sneered at her downed opponent and swiped at the hair falling in her eyes and faced Reo. "Let's go."

Reo shifted and moved her to the middle as he and Sora escorted her between them. Savie blew out a breath in disbelief. When they were some distance away, Savie said, "I'm sure Kelix wanted us to keep a low profile."

"We did," Sora answered with a derisive glance. "I made sure to leave a generous amount to cover our food and damage. The owners will stay silent. As to Kjar and his friends and the other customers, no one will talk."

Savie gaped. "You can't know that!"

Reo exchanged a glance with Sora and said, "She is truly naïve."

Chuckling Sora shook her head. "The customers had visible slaver tatts on their necks. Everyone that was in there is in hiding."

***

Savie had never been more grateful to finally return to the suite after the events at the eating spot. She remembered her plan to speak with Cy.

"Cy? Cyllus?" she called, going to the bedroom in search of him.

Unfortunately, he wasn't there. Nor did he come back by the time she fell asleep late that night. She'd talk to him in the morning.

Except the next day was the same. Cy was gone before she woke. Savie knew he'd come back because his scent covered the pillow beside her and someone had placed more items for her on the bedside table.

Toiletries, a few more clothing items, all in shades of blue. She blushed when she pulled out the delicate silken material at the bottom of the stack.

Underwear.

Chapter 19

Cyllus had barely spent any time with Savie over the last few days. Working behind the scenes to arrange a meeting and payment to the Andruvion with information about Earth had been a time consuming process. He'd walked away with another site to link for more details.

The good news was the relationship he sensed developing between her and Sora. The other woman took Savie out daily to keep her occupied. A friendship was growing there. Unfortunately, it wouldn't blossom further. Today was the day he'd get the final answers.

With Savie sleeping peacefully, Cy left in the morning with Kelix to meet the anonymous contact who'd answered his probe online regarding the Vassi and the deal with the Protectorate. When Cy arrived, another Andruvion stood against a shop wall in the alley adjacent to a bustling street, head ducked low to downplay his height. Standing at least seven feet tall in his boots, he would definitely draw attention.

Luckily, the Andruvion had chosen to dress in non-distinct clothing and an oversized cloak that hid the hunched way he carried his shoulders.

"Are you the one Botto said was looking for information on Earth?"

The Andruvion's language using hisses and clicks came through as clear words with the help of the translator. Cy spoke in the same clicks, the language available to his brain as if he'd studied it. "Yes. What do you have for me on them?"

The Andruvion winced at his poor inflections but nodded to show he understood. "No one is looking for any lost inhabitants from that world."

"What about an unauthorized research ship leaving the planet?" Cy asked.

More click and hisses. "Would be hard. Protectorate has assigned the Vassi as mentors to this new planet."

Except it had happened with Savie and her research team members.

"How long would it take a ship to reach Earth?" Cy asked.

"From Solus, twelve weeks. It's located in the opposite direction of the Eridani sector. Would be easier to go to Vassi. That trip is four weeks from here if you could hyperjump over to the Durajke sector."

A three month trip if he sent Savie back home, only one month if he sent her to the Vassi for sanctuary. The Vassi would welcome her with open arms and see to her care until she decided what she wanted to do.

Cy shied away from the fact both options took her from him and far out of his reach. He'd made Savie a promise to help her. His feelings didn't come into it. Cy paid the Andruvion and ignored Kelix's stare.

He should have known better. As soon as they were alone, Kelix asked, "What are you going to do?"

"There are only two options. She heads to Vassi or she heads to Earth."

Either would devastate Cy but he masked his feelings regarding that.

"You know that's not what I mean. I've seen you with her. You've grown close to this female."

More than close. She owned his heart. "Yes, well, that doesn't mean anything when weighed against her safety."

"Cy." Kelix gripped his arm and stopped in the middle of the street.

Cy tugged but didn't want to make a scene. He pulled the brim of his hat lower and bit off a frustrated growl. "What do you want from me, Kelix?! First, you said get rid of her because she was a hindrance and now you want me to what...keep her here?"

"I admit to questioning your logic at the time but it's become clear to all of us that she means something to you, Cy."

Everyone had noticed his feelings for Savie?

"Xion and Kaito mean something to me too. More importantly, my mother, Kala and my sister, Miri. Should I forget all about them?"

They were drawing stares. Kelix switched to their NNP. *"You're being obtuse. You don't have to choose one over the other."*

"You're wrong. I can't have it all, Kelix. I don't deserve it."

"Fucking idiot!" Kelix dropped his arm, walked off then stopped. He spun around and stormed back toward Cy. *"I'm all for finding our pod brethren but that doesn't mean putting your life on hold. Come on, Cy. You have something special with Savannah."*

He hadn't seen Kelix this passionate about anything since they'd discovered Shui had lied.

"I'm going to give Savie the choice on what she wants. I'll agree with whatever she decides and accompany her if she likes." Cy wasn't sure he could send her alone without confirmation that she reached her destination safely.

Kelix switched to verbal speech. "You're a fool, but it's your choice, and I admire you for making it even if I disagree."

They returned to their lodgings in silence. What he'd learned from the Andruvion weighed heavy on Cy's mind. Part of him hoped Savie chose him but Cy held out little hope of that.

Back in their suite, Savie was awake and dressed. She'd showered but the cleanser couldn't do anything to cover the smell he'd come to associate as purely hers. Cy walked up to her and pulled her into his arms. After she left, he'd missed being able to simply hold her.

He'd tried to get as much done as possible for fear their presence would be discovered any day. Yet more and more, he felt settled here. Everyone minded their own business and no one seemed on the lookout for renegade cyborgs on the run. It was a good place to pause and think.

***

Savie pressed her ear to his chest and Cy waited. She'd told him she liked listening to the hard thump of his heart.

After a few minutes, she tipped her head back to meet his gaze. Something troubled her. She rubbed her hands across his shoulders and leaned up to kiss his chin. He angled his face down and caught her lips in a kiss that stole his breath. When he pulled back, they both panted.

Lust clouded her gaze but Cy didn't want to be distracted. It was time they talked. He made his voice gentle and said, "I need to talk to you."

Fear darkened her gaze and he hated seeing it. "Is everything alright?"

Cy joined their hands together and led her to the backless wide lounge chair meant for an entire sports team to fit. Savie sat beside him and watched anxiously. Before he could explain the situation and offer her a choice on her future, she blurted, "I don't want to go."

"What?"

Savie squeezed his hand. "I don't want to go back to Earth. I heard you talking the other day and it sounded like you wanted me gone."

He cupped her cheek. "Savie, of course not. I wanted to fulfill my promise to you. I said I'd help find a way for you to return home and I did."

"What if I want to stay?"

"If that's what you want." She was killing him. His pulse raced and his breathing grew rapid. It was what he wanted too. "At least let me tell you what I've learned before you make that decision."

Her reply took a minute then she straightened and nodded. "Okay. Fine."

He took a deep breath then shared what he'd learned from the Andruvion. "This means you can go back to Earth, or you can go to Vassi and they'll do whatever they need to make you feel comfortable. I will go with you no matter what you decide."

Savie launched herself into his arms and Cy barely had enough presence of mind to catch himself before they both tipped over the back of the lounger. He tightened his arms and braced his feet on the floor.

The weight of her body against his felt right. Cy curled around her and buried his face at the base of her throat. He licked and nibbled her soft skin, enjoying how she melted from his touch.

Her breathy moans teased his ears as he stroked his hands up and down her back, following the line of her spine. Savie arched and rocked in his lap.

He trailed kisses to her lips and nipped at the corner of her mouth. Her tongue darted out and licked the seam of his lips. She kissed him in tiny increments, her mouth playing over his with soft touches. It reminded Cy of a specific journal entry.

"I'm a girlie girl sometimes and I love kissing. There's something so intimate and vulnerable about kissing. It tells you a lot about the person."

Cy hadn't understood when he first heard the words from Savie but now with her on his lap and their mouths tasting and teasing each other, he got it. He understood what she meant. Kisses were exploratory. They opened up a part of yourself you tended to withhold. It was an intimacy he'd never experienced. Even with prior lovers.

Each time he kissed Savie, he had these feelings and they only continued to grow. His heart ached as their tongues touched. With his mind full with thoughts of Savie, tension eased from his body in a way he didn't expect.

Rolling over, Cy lowered her to the lounge and crawled over her sprawled form. "I never dreamed I'd meet someone like you."

She grinned and tugged at his hair to pull him in close. Her words whispered across his lips as she replied, "Me either. I really like you, Cy."

A smile creased his mouth. "I adore you, Savannah from Earth."

Apparently, his statement tickled her. Her blue eye lit with laughter and her mouth curved upward. Pink blushes stained her cheeks and it was a look he couldn't resist. He dove back down to return to the drugging kisses. Savie slid her hands under his shirt and he groaned from the contact.

Skin to skin, he rubbed along her frame, wanting nothing more than to be one with her.

"Off. Take it off," Savie moaned.

Cy sat up and whipped it over his head, then eyed the shirt she wore with a wicked smile. Savie licked her lips in a slow taunt, pulled the shirt over her head and tossed it to the floor. Laughing, Cy leaned in close. He felt light inside and it was all because of this female.

He rose from the lounger and scooped Savie up in his arms. He carried her into the bedroom and put her in the center of the bed.

"Undress," he ordered. His voice gruff, the tone hoarse. He couldn't get his pants off fast enough as he watched for her reaction to the command.

Savie scrambled around and removed her pants and her shoes. The delicate lace underwear he'd brought her highlighted the damp patches on the front panel. Her inner thighs glistened with the arousal he'd brought forth.

"I'll remove those." Cy climbed on the bed and took up position over her. Hooking his thumbs in the sides of her panties, he slid them down her legs.

He ran his hands up Savie's thighs, appreciating the way she shook and trembled. Her eyes glazed over, her lips parted as he glided up to retake her mouth in a passionate kiss. He settled between the opening created by her spread legs and rocked his thick cock over her soft mound.

Wetness gathered and slicked his aching length, so he rocked again, hissing at the sensual contact.

"I want to feel you in me, Cy."

Savie's words were all the encouragement he needed. He pushed up to his knees and guided himself forward. The warm clasp of her opening swallowed the tip. Glancing down, he watched as he pumped gently until they were hip to hip and he was fully sheathed inside.

Eyes clenched shut, Savie moaned long and hard. Cy focused on her pleasure, driving their bodies closer and closer to the pinnacle. Sweat dripped down his back and Savie gasped beneath him. Together they raced toward the end until Savie broke first. She ground against him and Cy drove into her over and over, climaxing with the sight of the ecstasy on her face locked in his mind.

Chapter 20

Cy awakened abruptly the next morning, thanks to Kelix through his NNP. *"There's been news about the others. Meet us in fifteen."*

Fully coherent from the moment he felt the mental contact, Cy glanced down at Savie. She wanted to stay with him. Joy exploded in his heart and some of the tension he'd been carrying for days faded.

It would be hard at times. He had to continue searching for his loved ones but he wouldn't have to do it alone. Savie would be by his side.

With that thought in mind, he dragged a hand down her bare hip, eased the covers away and whispered her name. "Savie?"

Her lashes fluttered but she didn't wake.

"Savie," he called again in a gentle tone while leaning down to kiss the curve of her shoulder. Her skin was soft beneath his lips and tasted of a hint of salt from her sweaty exertions the night before.

Cy smiled. He'd kept her up last night and both of them had collapsed in each other's arms without showering.

"Savie, wake up. I have to go out for a bit."

Cy hadn't paid as much attention to it before but he realized she was often slow to climb from the bed and tended to stumble her way to cleanse and eat. Savie waking up was a process. She wasn't usually clear eyed until she'd moved around some.

His words had the effect of bringing her to conscious faster. The line of her back stiffened. He scooted lower in the bed and placed kisses down her spine, stopping at the jut of her hip. Caressing the soft flesh, he whispered, "Are you up?"

"Unh uh."

Another smile slashed over Cy's face. Had anyone else ever brought forth this level of amusement in him? "I'm meeting Kelix. He reached out to me that there is news about our pod."

Her head popped up and she glanced over her shoulder and down. Cy held her gaze and flicked his tongue out, licking the curved underside of a plump cheek.

Pink rose and spread from her neck to her upper thighs in a tidal wave. The scent of her awakening arousal tickled his nostrils. Savie turned over onto her back and he was sucked into the sensual stare she cast his way.

Cy slid up to give her a chaste kiss on her forehead. Savie looped her arms around his neck. "Do you have to go right now?"

The cheeky look on her face tempted him to blow Kelix off but Cy couldn't do that. There had been a sense of urgency to his friend's tone. "I'm sorry. Hold that thought for when I come back."

Her mouth turned down at the corners then she perked up. "Can I come, or is it a secret cyborg thing?"

Not wanting to be apart from her so soon after resolving their plans to be together, Cy kissed her quickly and leaped over her from the bed. "You can come. It will give me time to tell the others that we won't be going with the Andruvion vessel and that you plan to stay here."

At the door, he turned back and blocked the surge of desire at seeing her laid out on the bed unashamedly naked. "You haven't changed your mind, have you? Whatever you want, I'll do. I hope you know that, Savie."

She pushed up in the bed, every inch of her a work of feminine art. "I want to stay. I'll need to contact my dad at some point. Reassure him that I'm alive. When I first left, I told him there might be a delay in hearing from me but I don't want him to worry."

"Agreed." Cy didn't know how but he'd make it happen. No parent or child should be left to wonder at their loved one's fate as he and the others had to. It was a soul crushing feeling.

A look of hesitation crossed Savie's features before she stood and clasped her hands together. "I also want to make sure Earth is notified about my team. They're in preserved containment pods back on Algor 1. Or AB476, as you all call it. They need to go back home so their families can have closure."

That would be a little harder but Cy would work to figure out a solution. "It will be done."

***

Showering with Cy was an erotic experience. His hands were all over her. He claimed he needed to make sure she was cleaned completely. More intimate caresses from him followed and Savie was lucky not to have drowned from his ruthless efforts to bring her to orgasm.

"Under ten minutes," he said, eyes aglow with amusement while he panted with his arms bracketing her in the stall.

Savie could only laugh. As tight as the space was she wouldn't have thought it possible but Cy had managed. Now dressed, they exited their suite together. She reached out to hold his hand. He stared at their joined fingers and the corners of his lips turned up.

"Is this okay?" she asked.

His fingers tightened on hers. "Very."

They walked down the hall and stopped at Tagan's suite.

"We have a problem," Tagan snapped from the door of his room.

They didn't get a chance to ask what before Tagan stormed down the hall and banged on another door. Sora opened it with a glare. To Savie, she offered a smile. Savie felt like they'd made the first inroads toward friendship with their shared meal that fateful day. Sora even offered to teach Savie a few self defense moves.

Hearing Sora's story and knowing about her friend Thalen, who was severely injured, went a long way to softening Savie toward understanding Sora's gruff nature.

Kelix appeared standing over Sora's shoulder. "Everyone come in."

Once the door closed behind them, Kelix waved at the seats. Cy sat and tugged Savie down onto his lap. She flushed but realized the others weren't paying them any attention.

"What's wrong with you?" Sora asked Tagan.

The other man practically breathed fire. He jammed his fingers through his hair and snarled, "Reo's gone."

Kelix stiffened. "What do you mean he's gone?"

Looking up, Tagan glared at each of them individually. "I meant exactly that. When I woke this morning, he was gone.

He had to have left during the night. Neither of us sleep much but I...visited a female for companionship. When I returned, he was watching out the window, staring at the encroaching darkness.

"Since he's not one for talking and I'm not either, I headed to my room and shut down for the night. He was gone this morning when I checked his room across from mine. There was a data transmission on the old comp in our suite. Said he needs to find out what happened to his pod. Can't rest until he knows how they died."

Kelix cursed. "This just complicates things."

Cy chose to interrupt. "Is this why you wanted to see me?"

"No." Kelix shook his head, his face taking on a somber expression. "I have news of Xion and Kaito."

Cy leaned forward, curving his arms around Savie. "Reliable source?"

"Yes. I got this from Botto. He was leaving this morning but decided to give us one bit of information for free"

Cy rasped out his next words, "They're alive?"

Savie heard his hope and pleading. Fear that the other members of their pod were dead rattled his usual calm. Her breath stuttered as she waited to hear what Kelix had to say. She wanted this to be good news for Cy.

"They're alive. I only have rumors, but I plan to follow up."

"Did he say where?" Cy asked.

"Gladyx."

Everyone stilled. Savie gazed around, not understanding what had drawn such an intense reaction.

"The gladiator games," Sora muttered.

Cy's eyes widened in shock then his jaw bunched in fury. Savie still didn't understand. "What does that mean? Isn't it good that you know where your friends are?"

It was Sora who answered. "Gladyx is a cruiser that travels constantly. It's the host site for vicious games where money turns hands faster than you can blink."

Sighing, Savie leaned back against Cy's chest. "That seems smart on their part. They're not in one place and are harder to find."

"Not all contestants on the Gladyx are willing or volunteered," Cy said.

Now it made sense why there was an edge of anger riding all of them. If gladiator games were what she was thinking, it could be brutal for someone who didn't ask to participate. Cy's friends might have been forced into fighting.

Silence fell around the room as they thought through this. Savie ran her hand back and forth over Cy's chest. He was a solid weight behind her, his hands clenched tight until the knuckles gleamed white where they met at her waist.

"There's more," Kelix added.

Tagan pounded his fist into his open palm. "Are you serious?! What about Reo? Are we going to do anything about him leaving? Sounds like you two are only concerned with your pod and forget about the rest of us."

"You're an idiot," Sora spat. "I've found Thalen and as soon as he wakes, I plan to question him about our grouping. None of us are forgetting that this process of reconnecting could take a long time."

Kelix narrowed his gaze on Tagan. "This part is about Reo, actually. Or his pod grouping, to be exact. They're only rumors but two women credit their lives to three cyborgs who shoved them into an escape pod thus saving them from the explosions.

"We don't know where the emergency capsule took them but it couldn't have gone far. I messaged and tracked locations within a viable distance but its all speculation at this point. Allegedly the women found passage on a new vessel and refused to disclose where they were headed."

"He told us that last transmission on his NNP mentioned two women," Sora said and then kicked over a chair. "Damn fool."

"Fuck," Cy muttered. "If the bastard had only waited, he'd have known we might have more information on his pod."

Reo could have talked to the women and heard more. Perhaps learning the details of how they'd died as heroes would bring him peace. Instead, like a hard head, he'd vanished without a word.

"Don't worry. Reo would have had to leave on a travel shuttle. We can track where it went. Get his ass back," Tagan said

"Or maybe we should let him be," Sora advised

Tagan snorted. "You can say that because we found Thalen."

"There's two more from my pod missing, fool. I'm just unwilling to leave him alone to go chasing after a hot head who didn't warn us of his plan."

Kelix raised a hand. "Calm down, Tagan. You, Cy and I can take the ship and go while Sora stays with Savie and cares for her brethren."

Kelix caught the look Cy exchanged with Savie. Guilt caused Savie to hunch her shoulders.

"You're kidding me!" Kelix stomped across the room, turned and pointed a finger when he spun back around. "Tell me it's not what I'm thinking, Cy."

Cy exhaled heavily. "I want to find my mother and sister. I can do that better from a stationary place. Dragging Savie around also isn't the smartest when no one's supposed to be connected to an Earth human. Remember?"

"This is rich," Tagan said with another snort.

Sora looked around at all of them. "It makes sense. We can't stay on the run constantly. I'm not sure it's good for any of us. I understand Tagan wanting to keep looking for his pod. But I also understand what Cyllus is saying. We can make it work. Part of our time spent on Solus as a base and then take turns going out in the ship to find our family, friends and pod members."

Savie could have hugged the woman. She'd perfectly put into words what Cy and Savie wanted.

Kelix sighed. "I guess it wouldn't make sense for us to split up now. We'll try it this way and see how things go. Our base on Solus and periodic trips to follow up on leads. Agreed?"

"Agreed," Cy said.

Savie couldn't help grinning. She got to keep Cy and didn't have to go back to Earth yet. "Agreed."

They waited for Tagan who glared.

"Don't be a hard head," Sora growled.

"Fine." Tagan gave in and threw his hands up. "I'm in."

With an unmistakable gleam in his black eyes, Kelix rubbed his hands together. "First up, Gladyx."

"And Reo," Tagan cut in.

"Yes, he doesn't get to escape us that easy," Sora said with an evil laugh Savie wouldn't want directed at her.

Cy nuzzled Savie's hair. "You're staying."

"I'm staying," she whispered.

Epilogue

A plan had been hashed out and a week later, Kelix and Sora were ready to leave. A manual hack on a basic comp enabled them to create a legitimate reason for the two of them to join the Gladyx cruiser. Sora had secured a position as a repair mechanic on the ship and Kelix was going as an eager buyer looking to sponsor one of the fighters.

The roles would give them the perfect cover and justify their presence if caught searching unauthorized areas.

They'd decided leaving first thing in the morning was best. The crowds in the transport station were smaller and less beings to see them leaving.

"The distance will mean I'm out of NNP range," Cy warned Kelix as they stood in a small group waiting for the departure time.

That part of the plan set Cy on edge but they had no choice if they were to attempt to find Kaito and Xion.

"I'll comm whenever it's safe for updates," Kelix said.

Comms would be limited though for their safety. If something did happen to Kelix, Cy wouldn't find out until later.

Kelix pulled him to the side and after a glance at Savie who waved at him, Cy followed. Kelix gripped Cy's upper arms. "What's wrong?"

"I want to make sure you won't do anything reckless looking for Kaito and Xion," Cy admitted.

He wanted to find his brethren too but not at the risk of losing Kelix. Cy couldn't contemplate losing more of his family right now. Despite their checks and all the locator flags, he still had no information on his mother and sister.

"I'll be careful. You know I won't take risks," Kelix assured in a firm voice.

Cy breathed out heavily. Kelix was the most sound soldier and cyborg Cy knew. He had to trust in his friend's abilities. Worrying wouldn't do either of them any good. "Just be safe. You're my brother."

Kelix jerked him in for a firm hug reserved for few of Cy's acquaintance. The hold was tighter than normal. Kelix murmured, "Jax and Deuce would be pleased to hear you say that."

Jax and Deuce were Kelix's brothers who'd perished during the first wave of Emperor Shui's search to wipe out rebels. They'd been good males, friends to Cy and Kelix's entire pod. His heart ached at the reminder of their loss. A loss he could feel in its entirety thanks to Savie. Her love freed him of the emotional restraint placed on him as a cyborg.

Inhaling sharply, Cy squeezed Kelix one last time and pulled back. "You need to go so you're not late meeting up with the Gladyx."

Kelix smiled and turned. Sora hugged Savie and whispered in her ear. Whatever she said made Savie jerk away in surprise then burst into laughter. The sight relaxed the remaining vestiges of Cy's concerns. Sora would watch Kelix's back and the two of them would be fine.

Tagan stood off to the side of their small farewell group with his arms crossed and a glower on his face to match the belligerent stance. Sora approached and slapped him on the back. Her gaze narrowed and the look on her face was void of all levity. "Remember your promise, Tagan."

Cy and Savie had agreed to keep an eye on Thalen's progress while she was gone. To everyone's surprise, Tagan volunteered to have Thalen moved to his suite since Reo was gone for the unforeseeable future.

For some reason, he argued Cy and Savie didn't have the space or time to attend to the wounded soldier.

"It makes sense," Tagan had grumbled when everyone stared in shock.

So later this evening, Cy and Tagan would wait until the cover of darkness and retrieve their cyborg peer and bring him back to their suites.

"I don't break promises. Ever," Tagan declared now with a dark look.

Sora nodded. "I trust you."

Another round of goodbyes ensued then she and Kelix strode toward their designated ship and joined the queue of passengers.

Cy, Savie and Tagan watched the ship take off from the transport station until it was nothing more than a dot in the hazy sky. Tagan turned to speak. A frown cut deep lines into his face, his green gaze turbulent. "Remind me why I decided to stay?"

***

Savie chuckled. His stern demeanor wasn't as fierce as he liked to pretend. She looked to Cy, who answered. "Because Kelix doesn't trust you not to lose your temper and get sucked into a gladiator challenge."

Based on what she'd seen in the short time she'd known him, Savie could very well envision that happening. She cared about the cyborgs and didn't want anything to happen to any of them. Her heart already overflowed with worry for Reo and his unexpected disappearance.

She'd felt closer to him than the others, his protective behavior toward her inexplicable. Savie needed Reo to be alright. She could only hope he returned to them when he was able.

Tagan huffed and crossed his arms over his chest again. He didn't speak during the walk back. He didn't speak on the elevator. On the eleventh floor, before they parted ways to their separate suites, he finally said, "You're right. If I saw the way they treated the contestants in person, I wouldn't be able to control myself. I already want to choke Reo for leaving without a word. A stupid data transmission doesn't count."

He turned on his heel and slammed the door in their faces. Cy exchanged a look with Savie and they both muffled their chuckles as they proceeded to their own suite.

Inside, Cy spun her around and looped his arms about her waist. Savie placed her hands on his shoulders and met his gaze. She could get used to staring at Cy. He wasn't just gorgeous, he was kind and generous of spirit. And all hers. The last made her giddy inside.

"I've been wanting to tell you something for a while."

"Oh, yeah?" she asked, thinking it was more to do with contacting her father. He'd arranged for an untraceable transmission. Savie just had to make the recording and Cy would see that it got sent. She didn't want her father and friends worrying about her.

Tagan and Cy were going to make arrangements for the bio-units on Algor 1 to be picked up and sent back to Earth. At some point, she'd have to reach out to the Vassi and explain what the Elusans had done but she put that off for a worry to deal with in the future.

"Yes." Cy led her to the lounger and nudged her to sit.

The lounger was becoming the sight for all of their serious conversations. She'd mentioned it once and Cy got a wicked look in his eyes and tackled her on the cushions to make love to her. The moment had been sweet and romantic while wildly sexy at the same time.

Savie folded her legs up beside her on the cushion and Cy sent her a wink. She could only shake her head at his antics. His lips curled up in a grin that spoke of hot nights. He'd changed so much in their short time together. The man who joked and smiled at her was a lighter version of the one who'd saved her at risk to himself.

When he kneeled before her and clasped the top of one of her knees, she frowned. Cy held her gaze and spoke. "I know we've only known each other a short time, Savie but I want you to know how I feel."

Savie swallowed and couldn't stop her fingers from trembling in her lap. "Cy?"

There was a nervous treble in her voice. He lifted one of her hands and pressed his lips to her knuckles and held them there. In that moment, Savie remembered their first kiss. The one he'd given her the day they met. His mouth had been soft on hers but his lips chilled. Now they were full of warmth. Her heart hummed silently.

Cy raised his head but kept hold of her hand in his. "I love you, Savannah Monroe. I think I've loved you from the moment I heard your voice on the journal entries. I'd closed off a part of my heart after my transition. I didn't realize how disconnected I was until your private thoughts brought me back."

"Cy," she whispered again, blinking back the tears welling in her eyes.

This wasn't the first time he'd shared his feelings about the journals she'd made as a final goodbye but he'd never actually said those magic three words.

"I love you," he repeated. "I love you for your laughter, your warmth and for how you've accepted my peers when they were closed off and judgmental to you."

Savie pressed her free hand to her lips. "I love you too."

Her declaration came out part sob as she dove off the lounger and into Cy's arms. He caught her and tightened his arms as he always did when they embraced. Savie kissed him as tears streamed down her eyes.

"I love you. I love you. I'm so glad you heard my messages. I'm so glad it was you, Cy."

Their kisses were rushed, frantic. Cy worked to get Savie's clothes off, unconcerned with where they fell. Soon they were naked, Cy on top of Savie. He stared down at her. "You mean the world to me. I never thought I'd have love. After everything that happened, I definitely didn't think I deserved happiness."

Savie shoved back the waves of hair falling over his brows and tugged him down. "You deserve *all* the good things, Cy."

He kissed her nose, the curve of her cheek then down the sensitive slope of her neck. Savie rolled her hips beneath him, the touch of his erection between her moist folds, sending her pulse to double beats. Cy groaned and lowered himself until they were chest to chest.

"You're mine," he murmured, planting drugging kisses along her jaw line then moving back to her mouth.

Firm strokes along her side accompanied the kisses. Savie rocked into his touch and moaned his name. It was like this each time they came together. Cy gripped a thigh and slid into her in a single powerful stroke. Savie arched up on a sharp cry and clenched her hands on his shoulders. "Cy!"

He planted his hands on the floor and plunged in and out of her with every fierce glide. Gasps, sighs, pleas fell from Savie's lips. She worked her hips up and down, wanting to give back to Cy everything he was giving her.

On a rough groan, he choked out her name. "Savie!"

His body shook with his climax until he slumped against her. Savie hummed in pleasure as little zings continued to roll up her spine. "Told you we have our most important conversations here."

A sharp chuckle burst from Cy then his expression grew serious. He stroked the hair back from her face and curled her into his lap on the floor. "This is only the beginning. When my friends and family are recovered, we don't have to stay here. We can go to Vassi or Earth if you want."

She nestled her face along his throat. "Justice first. We have to find justice for you and all those on your world who suffered. After what your emperor did, he needs to pay."

***

Cy closed his eyes on Savie's words. She was the perfect match for him. He would have given up his battle for vengeance against Shui if she'd asked. He should have known better. He held her tighter and gave thanks for finding Savie and having her in his life. No matter what she said, Cy didn't know what he'd done to deserve her.

"Justice. We'll do it together," he said.

And search for his missing pod brethren and family.

Author's Note

I've never done a full on cyborg book and what a blast it was writing this. I can't wait to do more and dig deeper into the backstories of the other cyborgs we got to meet. Each one of them is tugging at me to do their story. LOL. I promise we haven't seen the last of these characters.

Making this experience even better, I got to team up with a great group of author peers and friends who have been such a joy and delight. Shout out to these wonderful ladies for pulling together to work on this project.

Up next is Her Cold Heart featuring my lovely lady cyborg. Woot!

For those who read *As Darkness Spreads*, you may have recognized a few similarities. Yes, those Vassi who are helping Earth are Venik's people, so you may get to see some series crossover at some point. For reference, *His Cold Kiss* takes place after *As Darkness Spreads* and will run slightly concurrent to *As Dawn Rises* which releases soon.

Scroll, flip and turn for a peek at Dawn's book.

As always, please consider leaving a review at whatever retailer you purchased the book from.

Happy Reading,

Michelle H.

As Dawn Rises-teaser sample

Venik and Sevanti studied Dawn through the two way view screen into the training room. The *jjaawirs* who'd been sparring had all stopped to watch her match with Calliope. Venik folded his arms over his chest and watched Dawn. For every one of Callie's actions, she countered with some odd move. He'd seen Dawn fight on Earth but this style was different.

"What is she doing?" Venik asked.

His best friend shook his head with a rueful grin. "I wish I knew. It's similar to our *knubtu* hand to hand combat using strikes, but she's throwing in hand stands and erratic flips that are taking Callie's timing off."

Venik agreed. One of the top decorated female *jjaawirs* on Sevanti's fighting force was being defeated by a human female seven inches shorter than her and forty pounds lighter.

"Has she gotten over her anger?" Sevanti asked.

Venik glanced to the side of him but his friend continued to stare through the view screen at the match. He didn't have to ask what Sevanti meant though. This latest topic was one of many that had created an air of discord between him and Dawn. "I don't believe so."

Learning she couldn't immediately return to Earth did not please Dawn and she made it a point to remind Venik she was here against her will. Unfortunately, Venik couldn't comply with her repeated requests. He'd given her nothing but the truth. Turning the vessel around before completing the mission wasn't an option.

"This won't end well," Sevanti murmured, drawing Venik's attention once more to the fight.

Frustrated with Dawn's speed and agility, Callie growled and charged. Her arms moved like whirlwinds—up, down, side to side, full body spin then kick. The kick was a surprise. There were no fighting maneuvers among their kind that involved body or leg work.

Dawn blocked the hand strikes, but the kick which Callie telegraphed should have been prevented from landing. Instead, it hit Dawn's chest dead center and she flew across the training room floor and fell flat on her back when she slammed into the wall.

Venik clenched his fingers to keep from stopping the bout. Dawn didn't stay down. The oxylilion armor someone had loaned her more than likely saved her from broken bones. She'd probably have bruises aplenty though. Callie had included a fair amount of strength in the kick.

More than was typically used in a practice or training session. Venik gritted his teeth on the curses he wanted to spew.

Using her hands as a spring board, Dawn thrust her legs in the air and flipped up back on her feet. The men inside let out a raucous cheer.

Venik's brow ridges rose. He hadn't expected that response from *jjaawirs*, their military's best. It was clear Dawn was a weaker opponent. She also fought against one of their own. He'd assume their loyalty would see them on Callie's side.

"They are impressed with the human. She has proven to be fearless and they admire her courage in battling against the odds," Sevanti explained.

"How many have challenged her?" Venik asked, wincing at the punch Dawn failed to block. A drop of red blood bloomed on her bottom lip, the right side of her face already bearing a garish pink undertone.

Her appearance was nothing like the Vassi with their copper bronze skin tone and tougher skin.

"Seven." There was no hiding Venik's surprise. Sevanti laughed at his expression and offered an explanation. "You are the one who gave permission for her to spar as a means to regain her strength."

He did. But Venik had expected Dawn to work with a training droid or take advantage of the combat holo programs. One on one fighting with this elite group was not what he had in mind.

Turning away from a particularly brutal strike delivered perfectly from Dawn to Callie's midsection, Venik asked, "Are they not concerned that she is a soft skin?"

The Vassi crossed paths with many races but humans seemed the weakest. Earth lacked the technology, weaponry and basic physiology of worlds much more advanced than them. With no natural defenses like claws, tusks or thicker skin, his people were already calling them soft skins.

Aptly named in Venik's opinion.

Callie yelped, drawing his attention back to the fight as she stumbled back under two rapid snap kicks to the face from Dawn.

"Are you okay?" Dawn paused and lowered her arms slightly to ask.

Fore ridges locked in a display of frustration, Callie screamed. Punching without care to style or skill, she launched for Dawn. Dawn's guard broke under the sudden attack.

She stutter stepped back with a grunt then danced away on a whirl and smacked Callie with a back hand to the face. Callie cried out, her bottom lip splitting on a crease of yellow but she didn't let the blow or blood deter her.

The women fought in a flurry of movements. The longer the match lasted, the more Callie lost her composure and Dawn seemed to steady. Rage coalesced on Callie's face at not easily defeating an individual she more than likely considered beneath her. It was easy to note the moment the tone of the fight changed.

No longer a battle of skills, the match shifted to a lethal dance that would leave one of them dead or severely injured.

"Call it," Venik snapped, rushing from the viewing room.

His twin hearts pounded a strumming rhythm as Venik tore down the hallway, the slam of his boots echoing loudly off the walls of the corridor. He burst through the door of the training room and came to an abrupt halt.

About the Author

USA Best Selling Author, Michelle Howard lives in a happy fantasy world where she writes sci-fi and paranormal based romances. Love stories have been a staple in her life since she discovered some of her favorite romance novels by classic authors like Judith McNaught, Julie Garwood and Johanna Lindsey.

I love to hear from fans so please reach out to me. If the mood hits you, leave a review.

Email: michellehowardwrites@gmail.com

Twitter: @mhowardwrites

Instagram: @mhowardwrites

Website: www.michellehowardwrites.com

Facebook: https://www.facebook.com/michellehowardwrites

Sign up for my newsletter via my facebook page or blog

Also by Michelle Howard

A Novel of the Dracol
Rylin's Fire
Relentless Fire
Frost Fire
Secret Fire

Assassins Guild
The Unexpected Bonding Vow
Claiming His Unexpected Baby
His Unexpected Mate

A World Beyond
Torkel's Chosen
Torkels Auserwählte
Arak's Love
Arak's Liebe
Lindsey's Rescue
Kyele's Passion

Rydak's Fall
Jaron's Promise
V'hor's Nestmate
Stolen Moments
Bane's Heart
Nikol's Surrender

Cyborg Redemption
His Cold Kiss
Her Cold Heart

Le Cœur dans les étoiles
Union à tout prix
Amour à toute épreuve

Liebe in den Sternen
Animalische Begierde
Einzigartige Liebe

Love in the Stars
Mating Urge
Love Like No Other

Magical Lovers
Djinn Lover
Wicked Lover
Wild Lover

The Vassi Contact
As Darkness Spreads
As Dawn Rises

Un roman de L'univers Dracol
La Flamme de Rylin
La Flamme verte
La Flamme de glace

Un Roman di Dracol
il fuoco di Rylin
Fuoco Implacabile
Fuoco di Ghiaccio

Warlord Series
Honor Bound
The Overlord's Heir

A King's Revenge
Rise of the Shadow Warriors
A Warlord's Heart
Unexpected Bride
Unleashing A Warrior

Wired
Wired for Love

Standalone
No Reason To Run
Project Genesis

Watch for more at www.michellehowardwrites.com.